Murder in Reverse

An Amy Bell Mystery

David Schwinger

PAGE PUBLISHING
Conneaut Lake, PA

First originally published by Page Publishing 2023

Although some named locations, such as City College, are real, all depictions of persons, events, and policies at any and all locations in this book are intended to be completely fictional.

ISBN 979-8-88960-044-2 (pbk)
ISBN 979-8-88960-052-7 (digital)

Printed in the United States of America

Also by David Schwinger

The Teacher's Pet Murders
Murder Spoils the Perfect Romance
Murder with Magic
Murder Takes the Top Prize
Murder on the Lido Deck
Letter-Perfect Murder
Willing to Murder
Retirement Was Murder
Reputation for Murder
Murder Couldn't Wait
Murder Makes Music
Murder Hits the Campaign Trail
Murder Saves the Day
Murder Finds a Way

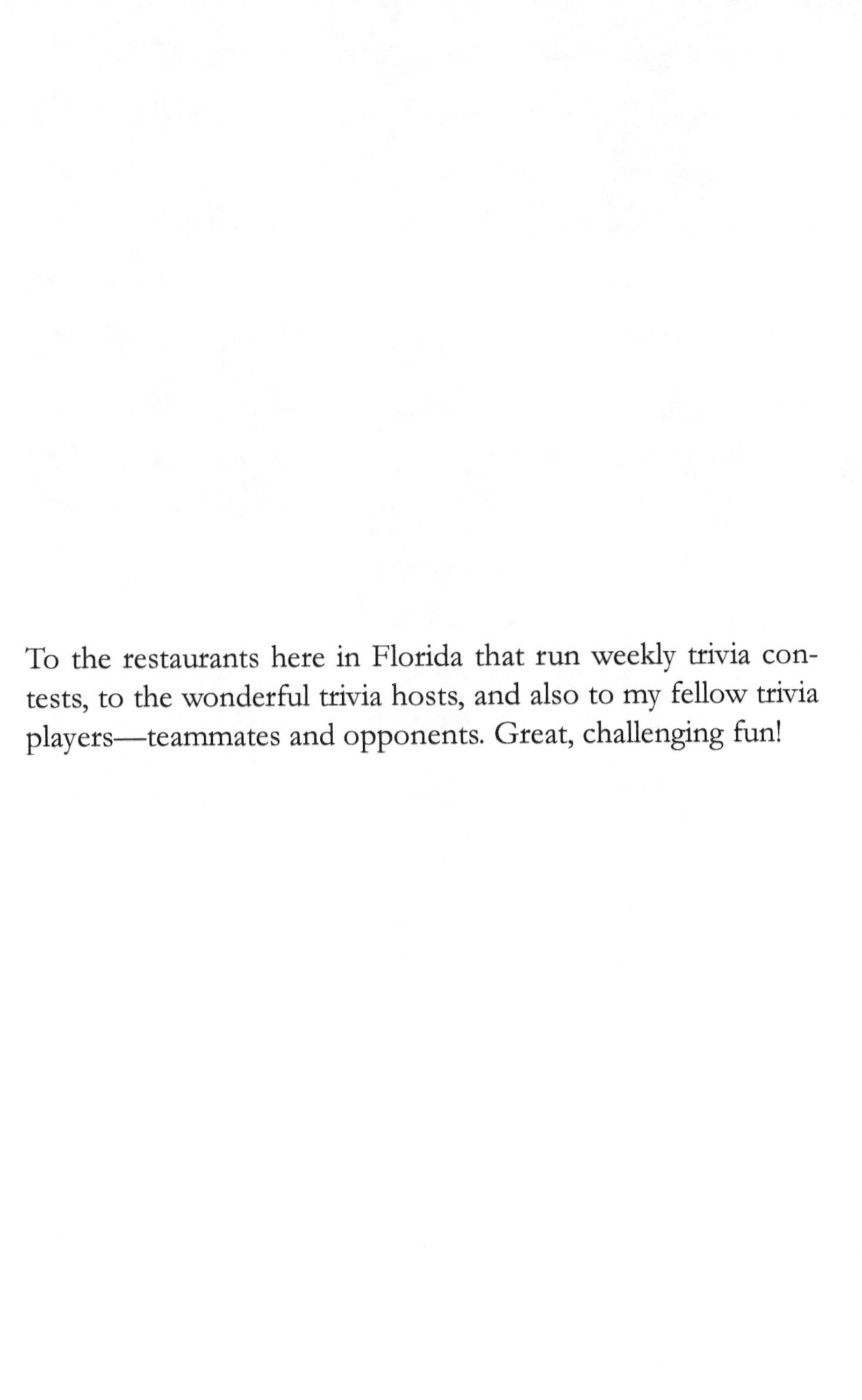

To the restaurants here in Florida that run weekly trivia contests, to the wonderful trivia hosts, and also to my fellow trivia players—teammates and opponents. Great, challenging fun!

Saturday, April 14, 2018

Mary Rackner was relaxing on a patio recliner in her backyard, facing her swimming pool, which she rarely entered except during the warmer months. She wore a sweater to be comfortable in the midfifties weather this particular midafternoon in Ferman Township, New Jersey. Mary's iPhone was set on Spotify, and she was listening to a medley of Whitney Houston songs, while periodically taking a sip from her glass of white zinfandel wine.

Beyond the pool—and outside the fencing which surrounded the backyard—was a thickly wooded area, and there was similar foliage on both sides of the house. Her property consisted of about half an acre. Visitors often told Mary that they envied the beauty of her immediate environs.

However, her thoughts on this lovely afternoon were not on relaxation-type topics. First, there was the Educational Excellence Project, which was so very necessary to preserve the nationwide reputation of the Ferman Academy. As a member of the board of trustees and also as chair of the project's advisory committee, she had come to what she felt was clearly the logical and reasonable conclusion about what had to be done, and she was sticking to her guns, despite some very passionate and vocal opposition.

And then there was the anonymous letter—the second anonymous letter—more threatening than the first letter. This new problem—to use a word that's much too kind—had arisen just recently. For now, she had hidden the new letter between pages 78 and 79 of her dictionary.

Mary had several options: she could do absolutely nothing, or she could do what she was currently considering, or she could make the maximum response in this situation. As she was thinking about these things, she began to succumb to the music and drifted, periodically, into and out of a nap.

Mary generally kept the gate to her backyard unlocked when she was out there, as neighbors would often drop by, both announced and unannounced, and she did not want to have to keep getting up to let them in and out.

So at 3:25 p.m. a visitor simply opened the gate and walked into the backyard, unnoticed by the snoozing homeowner. This visitor, wearing gloves, took out a handgun—equipped with a silencer—and shot Mary four times. The victim died instantaneously. The killer then tossed the gun into the pool and exited unobserved.

*****

With an abundance of suspects and a dearth of clues, the police were making no progress on the Mary Rackner murder case. Then one of Mary's best friends retained the services of a smart—and sexy—private detective who had to think far outside the box to expose the killer.

Tuesday, May 15, 2018, Morning

At 10:25 a.m., Amy Bell was relaxing in her office at Spy4U Services (located in Manhattan in the Forties, just off Ninth Avenue), where she was vice president for Sensitive Investigations. She checked her messages and perused the news, which disturbed her sufficiently to phone her husband, Jeremy Green, a freelance consulting actuary who generally worked out of their two-bedroom, two-bath Greenwich Village co-op apartment. Unlike everyone else, Amy called him Jerry.

Amy and Jeremy had been married for more than eight years. She told anyone who would listen that Jeremy meant everything to her. Before they first met, on a Friday evening in March 2007, at Marty's, an Upper East Side singles bar, she had been a self-ish, politically intolerant bully who made it a practice of insulting people who disagreed with her. Amy now freely admitted that this had been a part of her personality, and that marriage to Jeremy had, to a large extent, calmed her down.

As a matter of fact, during that first encounter at Marty's, when Jeremy told her he greatly admired Ronald Reagan, she flew into a tirade, accusing him of being—among other things—a reactionary and a self-hating Jew. Amy had been brought up at home to be a "progressive" liberal who cared about oppressed people in America and wanted the government to take all possible measures to promote equality. She proudly retained those politics as an adult.

But she was strongly attracted to Jeremy's classical good looks. At age 25, Jeremy was three years older than Amy and, at five foot eleven, seven inches taller. Amy was also drawn to Jeremy's modest, almost shy personality. Jeremy grew up in Columbus, Ohio, where he had very limited success with dating. He was not at all like the New York City men whom Amy generally met.

Amy wanted to take Jeremy back from Marty's to the Astoria, Queens, apartment she shared with her friend Cathy. Cathy was with Amy at Marty's that evening, and she had hit it off with Eddie, Jeremy's friend, who had accompanied him to the singles bar (Cathy and Eddie also eventually married).

But when Amy told Jeremy she was going to get her coat, he—quite reasonably—assumed she was a nutcase who hated his guts to boot and was now getting rid of him. He left Marty's by a side door and went home, alone and depressed.

But Eddie phoned Jeremy the next morning and convinced him to call Amy and give her another chance. Jeremy did phone Amy, and she invited him to come over to her apartment, and they would "go out somewhere."

But, in fact, they never left Amy's apartment that Saturday. What they did was make love—twice, with both events initiated and led by Amy. This resulted in a torrid affair that lasted several months, followed by a longer period where they were friends with benefits. Finally, in November 2009, they realized that they had loved each other all along, and they became engaged, with marriage coming two months later.

When people familiar with her politics asked Amy how she could have fallen in love with and married a Reagan lover, Amy usually responded that sometimes God smacks you in the ass and there's nothing you can do about it. Speaking of God, Amy described herself as Jewish and nonobservant but quite "spiritual." Israel was, in fact, the reason why Amy had phoned her husband.

"Jerry, your president—I try to avoid using his name—has done it again. Due to his ultra-reckless decision to kick our embassy out of Tel Aviv and unnecessarily impose it on Jerusalem, he has caused massive anti-Israel and anti-America outrage, lots of violence, and many deaths, with likely more to come. How can you support this vile, disgraceful man?"

Jeremy waited a few seconds before responding. "Sweetheart, I thought you were phoning to join President Trump, the whole nation, and me in expressing gratefulness for Melania's successful kidney procedure and joy that she will be able to leave the hospital in two or three days." He then began to laugh heartily. After hearing this go on for about ten seconds, Amy hung up in disgust. "There you go, God," she muttered, "smacking me on the ass again!"

Amy's thoughts regarding God's periodic smacking episodes were interrupted by a knock on her office door. It was her boss, Chester Murray, the founder and president of Spy4U. Nearly all employees at Spu4U called him Chester—at his request—but Amy generally called him Mr. Murray, out of respect for him being responsible for her career as a detective, rather than as a lawyer, which was her goal when she began as a political science major at City College (CCNY).

Amy's parents were not wealthy, and in the summer of 2003, Amy was looking for part-time employment to help her pay her expenses and enable her to stay in college. A neighbor told Amy that Spy4U had an opening for a part-time job during the mornings. Amy didn't have a resumé, but bright and early the next morning, she traveled to the Spy4U headquarters and waited outside Chester's office until he arrived. She told Chester that she would work as diligently as was needed to achieve excellence in every assignment.

It turned out that Amy's neighbor was mistaken; there were no job openings. But despite Amy's absence of any experience and her platitude-filled presentation, Chester saw something special in Amy and offered her immediate part-time employment. Amy was so excited that she neglected to ask Chester about her salary until she had been on the job for a week.

When Amy graduated from CCNY, she accepted Chester's offer of full-time employment at Spy4U. In fall 2009, Amy solved the murders of three fellow students in an evening adult education class she was taking. Amy's role in the case gained her some media publicity, and to make sure she didn't accept a job offer from a competitor, Chester promoted Amy to her current VP title.

Chester never regretted this decision. Amy had become a super-star at Spy4U. In addition to her detective assignments, she now supervised several other Spy4U people. Her specialty was solving murders that had stumped the police, some of whom now referred to Amy as "Sherlock Bell."

Amy invited Chester in, and they sat in comfortable chairs away from her desk. Chester immediately revealed the reason for his visit. "Amy, I just finished a phone conversation with Christine Longley, a former client of Spy4U in a marital infidelity case.

She ended up divorcing her husband five years ago and receiving a lump-sum settlement of twenty-eight million dollars.

"Christine lives in Ferman Township, New Jersey. A month ago, one of her best friends was murdered while apparently relaxing on a recliner in her own backyard. According to what Christine has heard, the police are making no progress on the case. She wants to hire us to attempt to solve the murder. Christine told me that since she now has no money problems, she owes it to her murdered friend to do everything possible to identify the killer and bring him or her to justice.

"Pending your approval, I have scheduled a meeting for two o'clock this afternoon for the three of us in my office. Of course, as always with murder cases, the final decision as to whether to accept the case is up to you."

Amy nodded. "No problem, Mr. Murray. I'll be there at your office for our meeting with Christine." After a few pleasantries, Chester departed, and Amy phoned her husband.

"Jerry, Jerry! I may be investigating a new murder case! I have a meeting at two o'clock today with a wealthy divorcee named Christine whose friend was recently murdered in her own backyard."

Jeremy knew how excited his wife always got about new murder cases. They made her forget all about her hatred of the current president. But he got in one final dig. "Sweetheart, whatever you do, don't tell Christine about your giant sexual crush on Trump, which is the true reason why you talk about him so often!" Before he could even begin laughing, he realized that Amy had hung up.

Tuesday, May 15, 2018, Afternoon

Christine Longley was in her early fifties, with a cute face and a plump but still modestly appealing figure—at least those were Amy's observations. After everyone shook hands, exchanged pleasantries, and agreed to use first names, Christine began discussing the reason she was there.

"I was friendly with Mary Rackner when we were both students at Rutgers. Her last name was Downey at that time. We lost contact after we graduated, and we rediscovered each other and quickly became very good friends when we both moved to Ferman Township—Mary in 2008 and myself three years ago. Mary's husband, Fred Rackner, died of brain cancer in 2013. He was independently wealthy through inheritance, and since their move to the township, he had dedicated himself to public service, including joining the board of trustees of Ferman Academy, a ninth-through-twelfth-grade private secondary school with a reputation for excellence."

Amy interrupted at this point. "Am I correct in assuming that Fred secured his appointment to the board of trustees by making a sizeable cash donation to the school?"

Christine laughed and nodded. "Good guess—ha-ha! Of course, Fred did have a background as an educator. In fact, he and Mary first met when they were both junior-level administrators at Fairleigh Dickenson University. By the time they moved to the township, Fred was doing public service as well as charity work, and Mary was becoming an author of children's books—even though she never had any children. Three of her books are on Amazon, all self-published."

"Christine," inquired Amy, "what made you and Mary decide, separately, to move to Ferman Township?"

"Mary and Fred were living in a gated community in Teaneck, and they decided they wanted a larger and more scenic property. Also, Mary had some sort of dispute with some neighbors—she never provided any details. I moved to the township to be near my significant other, Charles. We continue to maintain separate homes. Charles is the best man I've ever been with, by a mile, in every way." Christine flashed a giant smile.

"Anyhow, when Fred died, Mary was chosen to replace him on the Ferman Academy Board of Trustees. I wish she had never accepted that position. Then she would almost surely be alive today, and I would still have my best girlfriend.

"Two years ago, a minor trend, over the previous decade, of decreasing English and math scores on standardized tests accelerated at Ferman Academy. Also, a group of independent reviewers of the students' written work reported that their writing was generally deficient. An advisory committee, headed by Mary, was created and tasked to compile a report with analysis of why this decline had occurred and suggestions on what actions the school should take to reverse this trend.

"As Mary explained it to me, the committee determined that the reason for the decline was that the academy had 'enriched' their curriculum by adding classes in dance and theater as well as advanced classes—beyond the basic courses, which had always been offered—in art and music. These classes diminished the time students spent on the basics, namely reading, writing, and mathematics.

"To preserve the academy's reputation for academic excellence, Mary firmly believed that strong measures had to be taken immediately, starting with the fall 2018 semester. She convinced the other committee members to join in her recommendations, which were released this past February.

"Substantially more time had to be devoted to the three basics. To accomplish this, the entire dance and theater programs should be eliminated, as well as all the advanced art and music classes. Required summer classes were also suggested for students who were underperforming. Mary was well aware that these suggestions were controversial and would result in protests, but she saw no other alternative. The school's entire reputation for excellence was at stake.

"By early April, despite many angry protests by parents and teachers, it was pretty clear that the board of trustees was ready to approve the suggestions of Mary's committee when they met in early May. But then, on April 14, Mary was shot and killed in her backyard. Her dead body was found on her recliner by a neighbor who got no answer when he phoned, so he walked over to Mary's backyard, opened the unlocked gate, and went in. His call to 911 was at 4:30 p.m.

"Based on what I've been told by the police, Mary was shot four times. She died immediately. The killer threw the gun—which had a silencer—into the pool, where it was recovered by the police. They say Mary died between three and three forty-five.

"The police searched Mary's house, and folded between the pages of a dictionary, they found a threatening letter Mary had recently received. They determined that the words in the letter had almost surely all been cut out from the April 3rd and April 4th editions of the *New York Post*, which is widely available for sale in the township. The words were neatly taped onto the paper. The text of the letter was released, but not a photocopy of the actual letter. I took a photo of the text from where it was printed in the newspaper, and then I printed out the photo. Christine took out a sheet of paper and read from it:

"Hello, Mary. This is the second and final warning letter. You must immediately halt your disgraceful actions, or you will suffer the consequences. You will not know what hit you. To repeat for the last time, stop now or else."

Christine put down the paper. "I have an extra copy for you." She handed it to Amy, who had a question. "Did the police find the first warning letter? The letter you read said it was the second warning."

Christine shook her head. "No. As I understand it, they didn't find the first letter. Maybe it was milder, and Mary threw it out, not viewing it as a substantial threat. Unfortunately, that's where the police have stalled out. I have a friend in the Ferman Police Department who says they've made no serious progress whatsoever.

"I have lots of money, so I phoned Chester this morning and told him I want Spy4U to do whatever it takes to identify the killer and bring him or her to justice, if at all possible. I owe it to Mary to do this for her. Chester told me that you are the absolute best for this type of investigation, and that it's your call as to whether to proceed, so I hope you'll accept the case."

"I presume," observed Amy, "that the murder weapon was an illegal gun, and the owner cannot be identified, or else it was stolen from its registered owner."

"Right, Amy. As I understand it, the gun, including silencer, had been stolen. Captain Mark Zorkin, of the Ferman Township police, is a longtime friend of Charles, my significant other, and he told Charles to tell me he will be happy to assist any detective I hire in every way he can. So he will provide you with more information about the case."

Amy was contemplative for a few seconds, then she spoke, "Mr. Murray is very kind and generous to call me the absolute best."

"Amy, you *are* the absolute best," Chester interrupted. "Every experienced police detective in New York City who has any familiarity with your achievements would confirm that. Many people at the NYPD call you Sherlock Bell. You've solved something like twenty murders, most of which would almost surely have remained unsolved without you."

Amy's face turned red. "Oh my god, why did you have to mention that Sherlock stuff? Anyhow, Christine, based on what you've told me, the likelihood of me—or Sherlock Holmes or Hercule Poirot or anyone else—solving this murder is not very high. I'll ask the police captain about DNA and fingerprints, but I'm guessing they've come up empty on those. Everyone who vehemently opposed the suggested changes at Ferman Academy is clearly a suspect, and that's undoubtedly several hundred people, at the very least.

"However, with that understanding, I'll accept the case. That way you will be confident that you did the best you could for Mary. And, who knows? Maybe I'll luck out and solve the murder. I have some more questions. First, how old was Mary?"

"Same as my age, fifty-three."

"Christine, can you tell me a little more about yourself?"

"Sure, my former husband—I no longer mention his name— and I had two children, who are both grown up, doing fine, and currently living on the West Coast."

"I am in the same situation," interrupted Amy, "regarding our current president. I get sick whenever I mention his name, so I scrupulously avoid doing so."

Laughs all around, then Christine continued, "I work from home as a part-time retirement consultant for a large financial firm. Helping people navigate retirement gives me a lot of satisfaction."

"Would you agree that the murder was a hollow victory for the killer? As I understand it, the entire board of trustees was in agreement with the committee's recommendations. So Mary's death would not affect approval of the suggested changes."

Christine shook her head. "Well, it didn't work out that way. When they met last week, the board voted, unanimously, to delay their decision—and therefore delay any actions—regarding changes in curriculum for a full year, pending further review. No further explanation was given. It was a very brief board meeting."

"Oh my god," Amy blurted out, "they were probably afraid they'd be killed too."

Christine nodded. "That could very well be the reason. Of course, we're just speculating. You should definitely speak to Polly Medwick, the current chair of the board of trustees. She may come up with a believable alternate explanation for the delay. In fact, you should speak to all four of the board members; it's normally five members, but they haven't replaced Mary yet."

"Will do. Did the police release any information regarding the envelope the letter came in, such as the postmark?"

"Amy, you can verify this with Captain Zorkin, but I don't think the police found the envelope, just the letter. Or maybe they did find the envelope, but they want to keep it confidential for some reason."

Amy nodded. "So maybe the police also found the first letter, and they're not telling."

"Yes, that's possible too, I guess."

"And Mary never spoke to the police about either of these two letters?"

"Correct, as far as I know. Again, you can verify that with the captain."

Amy smiled. "Okay, Christine, you've convinced me. I've got to speak to Captain Zorkin as soon as possible!" Everyone laughed, then Amy had another question.

"Christine, do you find it odd that Mary never mentioned the letters to you?"

"Well, it's not really that odd. We did speak to each other frequently—several times a week—and we also often visited each other's homes. But my guess is that Mary probably didn't want to upset me. I can understand that. We almost always spoke about positive, upbeat things."

"Was the backyard wide open, or was it fenced, with a locked entrance?"

"It was fenced, but Mary often left the door unlocked. The killer likely just opened the door and walked in while Mary was already in the backyard and then shot her."

"Okay, Christine, believe it or not, I currently cannot think of any more questions. I always share all the details of my cases with my husband Jerry. He has often played a key role in helping me solve a murder. Is that okay with you?"

Christine nodded vigorously. "Sure."

"Great! As soon as possible, please confirm with me when Captain Zorkin has been informed that you have hired me and Spy4U to investigate Mary's murder. Then I'll make an appointment to speak with him. I'll take my leave, and Mr. Murray will go over all the details with you."

The women rose and shook hands; then Amy exited Chester's office. She returned to her own office and phoned her husband. "Jerry, Jerry! Game on! Go out and bring home a large pizza, with pepperoni and meatballs, for dinner, plus vanilla fudge ice cream for dessert. I should be home at around five fifteen. After dinner, I'll give you all the details of the new murder case."

Jeremy knew that this was no time to discuss his own personal preferences regarding dining options, pizza toppings, and desserts. "Sure, sweetheart, see you then."

Tuesday, May 15, 2018, Evening

Dinner was over, and Amy had just finished updating her husband regarding the murder of Mary Rackner. "So, Jerry, what are your first impressions?"

"Well, sweetheart, I suggest that you find out who inherits Mary's money. That person—or persons—would be my prime suspect. The letters were probably sent as a diversion."

"Don't you think Mary's suggested changes could enrage someone—such as a parent of a student taking dance classes—to the point where he or she might commit murder? After all, as you know, I had a previous case where a murder was committed to gain a benefit at school."

He nodded. "Yes, of course I remember that case, but there, the school-related benefit the killer was hoping to achieve was many orders of magnitude greater than in this situation."

Now Amy nodded. "Yeah, that is certainly true. Anyhow, I'll be sure to ask Captain Zorkin about Mary's will. To my mind, there are some glaring oddities here, assuming we have the facts right. First, Mary seems to have thrown out the first letter and both envelopes, but not the second letter. Also, Mary never contacted the police."

"Sweetheart, that does sound weird. I think the most logical explanation is that Mary did not take the threats seriously. She had recently received the second letter, and she would have thrown it out too, in the near future, had she not been murdered. Or, possibly, at the time of the murder, she could have still been mulling it over as to whether to contact the police, now that she had received the new letter."

His wife shook her head. "But then she would have likely kept the envelope with the letter and thrown them out together."

Jeremy was ready for that. "Maybe the letters were left in or under Mary's front door, or something like that, and there were no envelopes."

She shook her head again. "Wouldn't someone put the letter in an envelope, even if they were sticking it in—or even under—the front door? I know I would."

"So would I, sweetheart, but not everyone would bother with an envelope. You should ask the police captain if the letter was found in the dictionary folded in thirds, as would be the case if it had been in a business envelope. Of course, I'm assuming the letter was on a standard eight-and-a half-by-eleven sheet of paper. You also have to ask the captain about that."

Amy nodded. "Duly noted."

"And my idea about the will doesn't preclude someone with a different kind of grudge against Mary sending the letters as a diversion and then shooting her."

"Whet different kind of grudge, Jerry?"

He laughed. "I have no idea whatsoever. Hey, you're the detective."

Amy changed the subject. "Jerry, if the murderer did, indeed kill Mary because of the suggested changes at the academy, do you think that person is the parent of a student at the academy?"

Her husband nodded. "Either a parent or a current student. We know that many teenagers in this country have been able to acquire illegal guns."

"Bingo," interrupted Amy. "You and your idiotic Republicans are unwilling to support reasonable gun control legislation. So more and more people are getting killed. You should be ashamed of yourself!"

Jeremy laughed, which further enraged his wife. "Sweetheart, you have it all wrong. The vast majority of guns acquired by teenagers and by gang members are illegal or stolen weapons— but you already knew that, as you told me you were discussing a stolen handgun with Christine. Also, Trump is making it his mission to better control the southern border, so as to prevent all those illegal guns from coming in from Mexico."

"No, Jerry, on the southern border, your president is trying to keep out refugees desperately seeking asylum. He is doing this because they are mostly people of color."

Jeremy knew that further discussion of this topic was of no benefit. "Okay, sweetheart, let me get back to what I was saying. I can imagine the murder being committed by, say, a serious dance student—or their parent—who views their future qual- ity of education as potentially being wrecked. Also, there are teachers at the academy who knew they were gonna lose their jobs if Mary's suggestions were adopted by the board. But as I said, I think it is more likely that the killer is not among the obvious academy-related suspects, and the motive is something other than the suggested changes.

"I presume your first meeting will be with Captain Zorkin. After all, you have to verify the facts of the case, regarding the letters, the envelopes, and whether Mary spoke to the police."

Amy nodded. "For sure. I hope that beyond the stuff you mentioned, the captain will have found some kind of evidence that might help solve the case. Right now, I have virtually nothing to go on. I'm not optimistic about what the police may have found, but as I said, I can always hope.

"And there's a problem with your diversion theory. If the police found out about the letters, they would have likely provided some additional protection for Mary, making it harder for someone to murder her. Also, of course, if Mary threw out the letters without telling the police, there would be no diversion."

"Sweetheart, it would be the same if the letter sender was related to the academy. The sender's ability to kill Mary would similarly be limited by the added police presence."

"True, Jerry, but in that case, the letter sender was likely hoping Mary would change her position and modify her suggestions, so that it would not be necessary to kill her."

Now Amy flashed a wide smile and began to stroke her husband on the cheek. "I hadn't even been considering the possibility of the killer using the letters as a diversion until you mentioned it. Right or wrong, that was very smart. And you know how sexually turned on I get when you say smart things." Her right hand left his cheek, unzipped his fly, reached in, and located the target.

"I want you in the bedroom, with all your clothes off, within five minutes. I plan to sexually abuse your entire body for an extended period of time." She continued to expertly handle the target.

At this point, Jeremy was no longer thinking about the murder case. He very willingly followed Amy's instructions.

Thursday, May 17, 2018

At 2:15 p.m., Captain Mark Zorkin greeted Amy at the door of his office. They shook hands and took seats. Amy was impressed with his confident manner, but not so impressed with how he had clearly allowed himself to become quite overweight and out of shape. She figured that as the captain appeared to be around age 60, he was planning to retire pretty soon, so he no longer cared as much about his appearance.

"Amy—is it okay to call you that? And I'm Mark."

"Sure, Mark, please do call me Amy."

"Okay, Amy, I am aware that Christine Longley has retained you and your firm to investigate the murder of Mary Rackner. I am also aware that your husband assists you in your investigations. It's important that you understand and agree that with regard to any and all information that I provide which is not clearly available in the media, such information is considered confidential, and you and your husband must not share it with anyone other than Chester Murray, the president of Spy4U, whom I have already spoken to on the phone."

Amy smiled and nodded. "Yes, of course, I agree to maintain confidentiality. And I'm very impressed that you spoke to my boss. It was absolutely the appropriate thing for you to do, and yet most law enforcement people I meet with do not take the time to do it."

"I appreciate that. Mr. Murray told me a bit about your record of solving murders. I'm very impressed."

She laughed. "I presume Mr. Murray neglected to mention the murder cases which I failed to solve."

Now Mark laughed. "We all know that in the business of solving murders, no one with substantial experience has anything even remotely close to a perfect record. In any case we'll be very grateful for any assistance you can provide. We're at a sort of impasse at this point. I think the best approach is for you to ask me whatever questions you have. Then if I have some additional information I can provide, I will do so."

Amy nodded. "That's fine with me. First, tell me about the circumstances of the murder."

"Okay, sometime between three and three forty-five in the afternoon on April 14, our best guess is that Mary was napping on the recliner in her backyard, having left the entrance gate unlocked. The killer entered via that gate, apparently unobserved, approached Mary, and shot her four times, in the head and chest, with a handgun, which was then tossed into the pool. Mary died instantaneously. When we found the gun, we saw that a silencer was attached, which is likely why no one apparently heard the shots. There were no fingerprints or DNA on the gun or anywhere else.

"The gun, including silencer, had been stolen from its legal owner—who lived in Pennsylvania—three years ago. The owner had reported this to the police at the time, as one of the items taken during a burglary of his home.

"We did, however, find one additional piece of evidence in the backyard—and I remind you that this must be absolutely confidential. We discovered two clear shoeprints, both from the same shoe. We consulted with the appropriate people and determined that they came from a shoe that is manufactured in Croatia and generally only sold in Croatia, Slovenia, and Montenegro. It is, to the best of our knowledge, not sold on the Internet, but, of course, we don't know that for certain.

"It's a lady's shoe. If we can find a woman with some connection to Mary who owns that shoe, we probably have the murderer. But that's where the trail has ended for us, at least so far. By the way, the vast majority of stores in that Adriatic area that sell the shoes do not keep the kind of records that would enable us to determine the purchasers. Their transactions generally involve cash, not credit cards."

"Mark, did you check out Mary's phone calls, her emails, and her interactions on social media?"

"Yes, with no useful results. Mary did not post on social media. But there were many hundreds of posts there denouncing her proposed changes at the academy. Maybe a dozen posts supported her. But beyond denouncing, there was nothing that could be viewed as a threat."

Amy switched topics. "Christine read me the text of the warning letter you found at her house. That letter stated that it was the second warning letter. Did you find the first letter? And did you find the envelopes for either letter?"

"No, to both questions."

"Was the letter you found done on a standard eight-and-a-half-by-eleven sheet of paper?"

"Yes, it was. The words—which were sometimes comprised of single letters cut out separately—were from two editions of the *New York Post* from early April, and they were taped onto the paper."

"Was the paper folded into thirds the way it would be folded to be placed into a standard business envelope?"

"Again, yes. But we don't know whether the letter was ever in an envelope."

"To the best of your knowledge, did Mary ever contact the police—or anyone else—regarding the warning letters or any previous threats, of any kind, made to her?"

"No, to the best of our knowledge, she did not. And if Mary had contacted us regarding the letters, we would have viewed the threats in the letters as very serious and taken various measures to protect her, as well as trying to identify the sender."

"Have any members of the board of trustees—or anyone else associated with Ferman Academy—come to you to request added protection as a result of the murder?"

"Yes, Peggy Delgado, a board member, asked us if members of the board could receive additional protection. We discussed what we can do. That's all I would feel comfortable telling you at this point regarding that topic."

"As far as you are aware, is there any history, in this area of New Jersey, of anyone reporting the receipt of threatening letters regarding any topic at all?"

"To the best of my knowledge, no."

"Do you know who inherits Mary's money?"

"Yes. Mary had no close relatives. She split everything evenly among five charities."

"Mark, I think I've shot my load—no pun intended. Is there anything else you can tell me about this case?"

"Only that we've interviewed all four members of the board of trustees. I'd say they're all somewhat scared, and I don't blame them. I'm sure they're all grateful that you're working on the case, and they'll be happy to meet and speak with you. I'll give you their contact information; just give me a minute." Within a short period, he handed Amy a printout.

"Amy, you ask incredibly good questions. Have other law enforcement people—or any other people for that matter—told you that?"

She smiled broadly. "Some police detectives have said that to me, but the person who most admired my skillful questioning was my future husband, on our first date, when I asked him, after a period of flirtatious conversation, if he agreed with me that we should immediately make love."

That comment resulted in about thirty seconds of hysterical laughter from Mark. When he finally regained his composure, he had an observation. "You know, Amy, I suspect you may actually be telling me the truth!"

Amy continued her big smile. "Mark, that's all I would feel comfortable telling you at this point regarding that topic."

The captain recognized that Amy had repeated his previous statement—regarding police protection for board members—word for word, and he again broke into laughter, joined by Amy.

When they calmed down, he spoke, "Amy, I'm not supposed to behave like this. You're a bad influence. I'll bet you get suspects to like you and relax with you so much that they let slip some incriminating information. You are absolutely unbelievable! Anyhow, please keep me informed of your progress and feel free to contact me with any additional questions you may come up with."

They rose and shook hands; then Amy departed and drove straight home. Upon arrival, she hugged her husband and excitedly provided the big news. "Jerry, Jerry! There are two lady's shoeprints—from the same shoe—in Mary's backyard! They're from an uncommon brand of shoes, only available in three Adriatic countries!" They proceeded into the kitchen.

"So, sweetheart, I presume that means the murderer is very likely a female, right?"

"You bet, and if they find the shoes, they've almost certainly found the killer."

"But they can't just go around and search everyone's house—and there's hundreds of houses to search—without justification."

"Right, it's called 'probable cause.' So the police are currently at an impasse. We were correct in surmising that the police did not find any envelopes, nor the first warning letter. Also, Mary never contacted them about the letters. Mark—Captain Zorkin—also confirmed that the letter they found was on a standard sheet of paper and was folded in thirds, as would occur if it were in a business envelope."

"Sweetheart, the killer may have realized there were footprints and therefore may have gotten rid of the shoes."

"True, but hopefully she didn't. Also, if she used some sort of gloves—which is likely as the police found no prints or DNA— she should have gotten rid of them, and my guess would be that she did."

"Couldn't the killer be a man who brought along a lady's shoe to make some prints in the backyard and fool the police?"

His wife smiled. "It's possible, but I'd say it's extremely unlikely. And regardless of the silencer, the killer would want to get out of there as fast as possible. But one thing is for certain now; you would make a great, wily murderer. I'd better be sure to remain on your good side!"

They both laughed, then Amy continued, "Regarding the will, Mary split everything among five charities. So that looks like a dead end."

Jerry nodded. "Well, I tried. Where do you go from here?"

"As Christine had suggested, I want to speak to all four current members of the Ferman Academy board of directors, starting with the chair, Polly Medwick. Beyond that, I'm not sure what I'm gonna do. I'll contact Polly tomorrow morning and try to get an appointment with her as soon as possible. Oh, what the heck, it's only twenty past four. I'll try to contact her now. Mark gave me the contact information for all four board members."

Amy went into the living room and made two phone calls. She returned to the kitchen shortly thereafter with the news. "I have an appointment to see Polly at eleven forty-five in the morning tomorrow. I'll also be seeing another board member, Peggy Delgado, at noon on Saturday; she specifically requested that day. Both of them requested to meet with me at the same restaurant and to join them for drinks and lunch. So it looks like now I know what is the go-to eatery in Ferman Township. Anyhow, game on!"

Friday, May 18, 2018

When Amy arrived at the Ferman Country Diner, Polly Medwick was already seated at a booth, to which the hostess escorted Amy. Polly rose and shook Amy's hand; then they sat down and ordered drinks. Unlike Polly, Amy ordered a nonalcoholic drink, namely a Coke Zero. They also ordered their food dishes, consisting of salmon for Polly and a burger plus fries for Amy.

Polly was tall and very slender; Amy knew she was fifty-five years old and had never been married. She observed the stern, serious look on Polly's face and decided that Polly would definitely not take any kind of crap from anyone at any time.

"Amy, I know I speak for all the board members when I tell you how grateful we are to you for accepting the case. I know that Christine Longley is paying you, but I did some web research regarding you and your career, and I know that you can take your pick of which cases you choose to work on. There seems to be a good chance that the police will never get anywhere, so you are our best—and probably our last—hope for solving Mary's murder. All the board members would like you to address them by their first names, and we hope we can call you Amy, as I just did."

Amy nodded. "Yes, Polly, by all means, please do call me Amy. Thank you so much for the kind words. I'm very happy to help the police in trying to solve this murder, but please understand that solving murders like this is generally a long-shot proposition. Of course, I'll do everything I possibly can. Captain Zorkin suggested, when I met with him, that the best approach was for me to throw questions at him. May I do that with you?"

"Sure, Amy, that's the way I expected this would go."

"Okay, who appointed all of you to the board of trustees? In other words, who is the ultimate authority over the Ferman Academy?"

Polly smiled. "That's a good question. We are one of several secondary schools around the country supported, financially, by the Great Education Foundation, run by Gerald Barron, who made several billions of dollars by selling a few Internet startups he had created. Gerald strongly believes that the bedrock of a high-quality education is ensuring excellence in reading, writing, and mathematics. The schools he supports must commit themselves to that.

"Because of this arrangement, we have a low tuition, and our teachers are very well-paid. We can always benefit from any additional funding, beyond what the foundation and tuition provide. Therefore, we are very grateful for donations from our wonderful friends and alumni in this community and elsewhere.

"Other than the three basics, the school has great leeway in its choice of academic offerings. Due to the falloff in the scores in those basics, we have been informed that our financial relationship with the foundation is in jeopardy, so we do, indeed, have to make some changes."

Amy interrupted. "So does the foundation appoint the members of the board of trustees?"

"Yes, as long as we have this financial relationship, the foundation selects the board members, and the members of the board elect a chair every two years. I have been chair since September 2015, which was only three months after I joined the board. No one else had wanted to be chair. I was reelected last September. We are paid a nominal annual salary which would not support someone for even one month. We do it because we care. When there is an opening, the foundation chooses from the list of people who have submitted a resumé and a letter of interest in the board position."

"Polly, what background do you have that caused you to apply and be selected for a board position?"

"My father, Adam Medwick, was a high-school principal and, prior to that, an English teacher. I taught high school English and creative writing, served as department chair and assistant principal, and then, in 2011, I changed careers, to some extent, and became education editor at a local newspaper. I still have that position, but on a part-time basis since 2014. In that year, my father passed away and left me enough money to have no problems in that area. I also still do some private tutoring."

"What would happen if the academy lost its financial support from the foundation?"

"If we could not secure similar funding from another source, my guess is that the school would end up shutting down, as I don't think substantially raising tuition would prove to be successful in attracting enough families willing to pay the much higher amount. Or, possibly, the academy could be annexed as part of the township's public school system, but I wouldn't count on that."

"Polly, I understand that the board recently voted to do further study and defer a vote on any and all curriculum changes until next May. Was this mainly due to Mary having been murdered?"

"No and yes. No, we did not vote to do further study because we were afraid of being physically attacked and possibly killed. By the way, the vote was unanimous, four to zero. We did speak to the police about them providing us with additional protection. But yes, it is true that Mary was, by far, the strongest proponent on the board of the draconian changes her committee proposed. She had done lots of research and analysis, and we had done very little if any. For that reason, plus Mary's enthusiasm, she convinced us that the future of the academy required the immediate adoption of all the suggestions of Mary's committee.

"After Mary died, we did a lot more thinking on our own, and we all ended up agreeing that maybe we could improve the students' performance in the basics without throwing the baby out with the bathwater, as the saying goes. We spoke to the foundation people prior to our vote, and they accepted our new plan, including the time frame, setting a vote by the board for next May on what will likely be a substantially revised proposal.

"I know some people will say the murderer got what he or she had wanted to achieve by killing Mary. But our job on the board is to make the best possible decisions for the welfare and success of the academy. And that's what we're trying to do. We've asked the school principal, Anna Morgenson, to put together an alternative proposal to that of Mary's committee, as well as to report to us on any other proposals which may have been submitted to her by others. You should speak to her."

"I sure will. I presume the school is coed, right?"

"Yes, right now it's about fifty-eight to forty-two, girls versus boys, which makes many of the boys very happy." They both laughed. "There's been a discussion regarding whether some sort of affirmative action would be a good idea to get more boys."

"Do you bus students to and from school?"

"Yes, more students than not live too far away to walk. Some are from nearby towns, attracted to the academy by its reputation."

"Polly, based on my last question, I guess you've figured out that I've run out of good questions." They both laughed heartily. At this point, lunch arrived, after which they said their good-byes and Amy departed for her Spy4U office.

A few minutes after she arrived, she phoned her husband and recounted her interview with Polly. "So I learned a lot from Polly about the school, the foundation bankrolling the school, and the current thought process regarding changes in the curriculum."

Jeremy laughed. "Yeah, but one thing is very obvious to me. Polly is lying through her teeth! You couldn't have really expected her to tell you the truth, that they're all scared wit-less—I'd use another word, but I'm in mixed company—about getting murdered, and they hope that during the coming year, prior to the vote next May, Mary's killer will be identified and brought to justice. In that case, they will not be afraid to make whatever changes need to be made."

Amy wasn't so sure. "Jerry, of course you may be right, but it's not as clear as you make it out to be. I think Polly gave a very reasonable and believable alternative to your scenario. As the head of the committee that did all the research, Mary had moral and knowledge-driven authority. The rest of the board naturally was prone to go with her conclusions. With Mary gone and her strong, authoritative voice silenced, the other board members psychologically felt more freedom to think for themselves."

"Sweetheart, those are a lot of fancy words used to cover up three simple words: they are lying!"

"So, Jerry, why don't you now tell me what you really think?"

They both broke into laughter, then her husband spoke, "On another topic, I'll bet all the board members turn out to be rich. I guess that's no surprise, given the minimal salary."

"I think you're right, and it does make sense. I'll find out for sure when I interview the other three board members. Polly suggested I also speak to Anna Morgenson, the school principal. She will be putting together an alternate proposal."

"Well, sweetheart, the principal wants to save as many teaching jobs as possible, so she may not be the perfect source for a viable alternative proposal."

"Sure, Jerry, but she does not want the academy to be forced to close. And Polly thinks that if the scores don't rise, that's a serious possibility."

"You do have a point there. Maybe I should adjust my thinking regarding the principal."

"Well, I certainly do want to speak to her, after I finish my interviews with all the board members. And I also want to find out what was the dispute that Mary had with some of her neighbors when she was still living in Teaneck. Christine mentioned that Mary had told her about the dispute without providing any details."

Amy hung up a few minutes later. At 3:15 p.m., she received a call from Cathy Mitchell, her best girlfriend for over a decade. Cathy had gone to Marty's with Amy on the evening when Jeremy and Amy first met. She met Jeremy's friend Eddie Mitchell on that same evening, eventually married him (a few months after Amy married), and they now lived in the same Astoria apartment Amy and Cathy had shared prior to Amy marrying Jeremy. Eddie was a detective in the NYPD, and Amy sometimes requested his assistance regarding an aspect of one of her cases.

The Mitchells had a four-and-a-half-year-old daughter, Aurora. Amy and Jeremy considered the Mitchells to be like family. After some small talk, Cathy presented an invitation.

"We just discovered that the regular Saturday evening singer/ pianist at Armando's Restaurant cannot be there tomorrow. It's too late for them to get a replacement, so they're running a Name That Tune contest in conjunction with a special buffet dinner. They will have a DJ doing the contest, and then he will play recorded music for dancing. The entire event is from six to ten tomorrow evening.

"Can you join us? They say the songs will be from the 1950s through the 2010s. You know the early stuff, because your father was a big doo-wop fan. I know the later stuff. The men know… well, they know whatever they know." They both laughed. "Armando's is a ten-minute walk from our apartment. As usual with this kind of thing, my mother will sit with Aurora. You should get here at around five. Then at quarter to six, we'll do a slow walk to Armando's."

Amy did not hesitate. "Sure, sounds like a lot of fun! Jerry usually plays tennis for about two hours, midday, on Saturdays, but I know we're free for tomorrow evening. And I just started investigating a new murder case. I'll give you and Eddie a few details tomorrow at dinner."

With that, the phone call ended, and Amy phoned her husband. "Jerry. Jerry! We're going to a Name That Tune contest tomorrow evening!" She gave him the details.

"Sweetheart, I hope you can control yourself this time and refrain from rising and protesting the answers. I still recall the last trivia we went to. The other teams were booing you."

"Jerry, I'll make every effort to control myself. But this is different from trivia. There should be no controversy, when they play the song, as to what is the title. I am very confident that there will be no issues for which I'll have to control myself."

After they got off the phone, Jeremy smiled and muttered, "No controversy, no issues. I'll believe that when I see it!"

Saturday, May 19, 2018, Afternoon

When Amy entered the Country Diner at five past twelve, Peggy Delgado was sitting on a couch near the front door. She rose and shook Amy's hand, then they were escorted to a booth. Peggy was sixty-three years old, short and quite heavy. They put in their orders, and Peggy started the conversation.

"Amy, you're likely our only hope to solve Mary's murder. I spoke to Captain Zorkin of the Ferman PD, and I could tell by the way he spoke and the look on his face that they're very pessimistic about finding the killer.

"But he could see that I was very scared, and he did agree to set up some special protection for all four of us board members. He has indeed provided this protection; however, I am not supposed to comment further on that."

"Of course," Amy interrupted, "that's understandable."

Then Peggy continued, "But how long can they maintain this added protection? Weeks? Months? Years? Don't tell anyone, as I have not yet made the announcement, but I will be resigning my position on the board as of this coming June 30, regardless of whether Mary's killer is arrested.

"Amy, I've been a secondary school teacher, department chair, assistant principal, and principal. I retired in 2015 after a lifetime of service as an educator. Now I'm a trustee for the academy. But I didn't sign up for something like this. Sorry, but I'm not going to wait until the police cut back their protection, and Mary's killer—or the next angry violent person—finds their opportunity to strike again."

Amy nodded. "I understand completely, and I'll certainly keep your decision completely confidential. Do you feel the board members were correct in delaying the vote until next May, pending further study?"

"Yes, regardless of the murder. Given how drastic Mary's suggestions were, we owed it to the academy, its teachers, and its students to carefully review all possible alternatives. And while I won't be participating, I'll bet the board finds a good alternative that preserves the arts and also provides the needed extra time and support for the basics."

"Are you surprised that the text of the warning letter to Mary was released by the police to the public?"

"Actually, Amy, someone leaked to the media that the police found, in Mary's house, a highly threatening warning letter addressed to Mary. At that point, with the cat out of the bag, the police released the text of the letter."

Amy nodded. "Now it all makes sense. Of course, most people probably assumed, even without knowing about the letter, that Mary was killed because she was the leading advocate for the proposed changes at the academy."

Now Peggy nodded. "For sure! Almost everyone has made that assumption, including myself. What other reasonable explanation could there be? After all, they said the killer used a silencer on his or her gun, so it was carefully planned and wasn't a random killing. The letter basically just confirmed what we already knew."

They enjoyed their lunch, then Amy drove home and waited for her tennis-playing husband to return. He showed up at two forty-five, and she gave him all the news regarding her interview with Peggy. "So the police might not have ever revealed the existence of the warning letter—let alone the text—had its existence not been leaked to the media. Before you got home, I did a web search and verified that there indeed was a leak."

"Sweetheart, I'm not surprised. I didn't mention it to you, but I had serious doubts that it was standard police procedure to publicly reveal that kind of thing. I guess I was correct."

"Jerry, I wonder why the captain didn't inform me about the leak, and whether the policy is to not publicly reveal such things as the warning letter. I can see the arguments both ways regarding whether to publicly reveal the letter. I should contact Mark and bring this up.

"And you have to take a shower and get properly dressed up and ready to leave here at four fifteen to drive to the Mitchells' house and then go from there to Armando's for dinner and Name That Tune. You don't have that much time, so get a move on!"

Her husband smiled. "Given what you just said, I have a music trivia question for you. Who had a top 100 hit in the US with the song 'Get a Move On?' I'll bet you don't know."

Amy laughed. "You win your bet. I have no idea whatsoever. I don't think I've ever even heard that song."

"Well, it was Eddie Money."

"Didn't he do 'Take Me Home Tonight?' That's probably his only song that I would be familiar with."

Jeremy nodded. "Yes, Money hit the top ten with 'Take Me Home Tonight.' He also had several other top 10 hits. Anyhow, I'll quit now while I'm ahead and take a shower."

Amy smiled. "Good idea."

Saturday, May 19, 2018, Evening

When they arrived at the Mitchells' apartment, at five o'clock, Amy and Jeremy knew what they would be doing for most of the next forty-five minutes, namely fawning over Aurora. They gladly fulfilled this obligation, which lasted a bit longer than planned, and they also exchanged pleasantries with Cathy's mother. The foursome then undertook their leisurely stroll over to Armando's, arriving at ten past six, where they were escorted into the banquet room, which was set up for the buffet. They were seated at a table for four, where they ordered drinks.

They observed that there were twelve tables set up for the participants, seating either six or four. Many were already occupied. At six fifteen, the buffet opened, providing a nice choice of dishes. Jeremy went for the sliced roast beef, while Amy chose the spaghetti and meatballs, with an abundant number of the latter.

During dinner, Cathy asked Amy if she could discuss this new murder case she was working on. Without giving any confidential details and referring to Mary as Barbara, Amy described her investigation. "So there might be some incriminating evidence, but unless the police can search hundreds of homes, they'll never find it. And that's where I am at this point."

Eddie immediately made an observation. "I'm pretty sure that absent the leak, the police would not have revealed the existence of the letter. If it was our case, barring very unusual circumstances, we would not have done so."

"So," asked Cathy, "after you interview all the board members and school officials, and maybe some highly vocal protesting parents, where do you go from there?"

Amy shook her head. "I have no idea. And why should a protesting parent even speak to me? I'm learning lots of interesting information, but nothing that would help me solve the murder. Even though it's still an early point in my investigation, I have this awful feeling that not only will the killer get away with it, but the killer's goal—namely to have the board veto Barbara's proposed changes—will likely be achieved. Of course, I'm not saying Barbara's proposal should actually have been approved; that's way beyond my pay grade."

Jeremy chimed in, "I've been saying, all along, that I believe the letter was just used by the killer as a distraction. I think the motive was completely different from the school issue."

"Why do you say that?" Eddie asked.

Jeremy smiled. "Let me count the reasons. The most obvious is that Barbara was the leader and prime mover of the controversial proposal. She wasn't gonna change her position. So why send a letter? Why not just kill her? Also, if Barbara gave the letter to the police, they would likely provide her with additional protection, making it harder for someone to murder her. And the letter might theoretically give the police some evidence with which to identify the sender."

"Oh my god, Jerry," blurted out his wife, "I'm so impressed with the way you presented all that! You're so smart!" She smiled at Jeremy and licked her lips. Of course, he knew exactly what this meant, but obviously, it would have to wait until they returned home.

"Amy," inquired Cathy, "do you agree with Jeremy that there's a good chance the letter was sent to hide the real motive?"

She shook her head. "No, I do not agree. Jerry is overthinking this. The killer is probably not that thoughtful and sophisticated."

"Well," interjected Eddie, "the killer was sophisticated enough to use a silencer."

Amy nodded. "Yes, you do have a point about that. Anyhow, regardless of the motive, I'm very pessimistic about solving this case."

Cathy had another question. "What about your other past murder cases? Were you generally confident early in your investigation that you would eventually solve them? Or were you usually pessimistic, as you are now?"

"You know, that's a great question," announced Jeremy. "And I'll answer it. Amy is almost always pessimistic during her murder case investigations, right up to the moment when she gets the brainstorm that solves the case. Sometimes, I say something which seems totally insignificant, and suddenly Amy tells me I just solved the case for her. Eventually, she lays it all out for me, but until then, I'm usually completely in the dark."

They enjoyed their desserts, and at 7:10 p.m., the host for the evening took the stage. "Hello, everyone, I'm DJ Music Maker—before you ask, no, that's not my real name—and I'll be setting up your dance music later on, but first, we're gonna play Name That Tune. Here are the rules:

"Each table must play as a team; please select a captain to make the final decisions regarding your answer sheet. There will be two types of questions. For each of the first twenty questions, I will play part of a song—a part that does not contain the title. You will get one point for providing the title and one point for giving the performer, which could be a single person or a group.

"For the title, you must have it exactly correct, except spelling does not matter, provided it is totally obvious what word you were intending to write. If you have any extra or missing words, you are wrong. If some part of the title is in parentheses, do not include it. For example, for the song 'December 1963 (Oh, What a Night)' you must write only 'December 1963.'

"For each of the final ten questions, I will read a line—or possibly only part of a line—from a song that was a top 10 hit in the US. For one point, all I want is the title of the song, not the performer.

"So there will therefore be a total of thirty questions, worth a total of fifty points. At the end, I will collect the answer sheets and grade them, which won't take more than fifteen—or at most twenty—minutes. Then I will go over the answers. Finally, I will return the papers and hand out the gift card prizes for the top three tables. I will explain my tie-breaking procedure only if it becomes necessary.

"Finally, no cheating! Put away your iPhones, et cetera, and don't yell out any answers, whether you think they are correct or incorrect." Laughter all around. "Also, the decision of the judge is final, and I am the judge. Is everyone ready? Then let's get this under way!"

Knowing Amy, the other three at the table were all very confident that Amy would immediately assume the role of team captain and take control of the answer sheet, which she did. As the game progressed, they felt they were doing pretty well, with Amy, as expected, specializing in the oldies.

When they got to song number 17, all four immediately recognized the lovely melody and the initial words, "Tonight you're mine, completely." The DJ stopped it after the second line, and Eddie proudly whispered, "It's 'Will You Still Love Me Tomorrow' by the Shirelles."

Everyone nodded, except Amy. "Right performers, wrong title. The word *still* is not in the title. It's 'Will You Love Me Tomorrow.' Most people get that wrong. Luckily, I'm not one of them." She flashed a broad smile.

For song number 23, the DJ read the line, "There's always pain in my heart." The other three had completely blank looks on their faces. "Shame on you, guys," admonished Amy. "You all know this song! It's 'Please Please Me,' by the Beatles." But none of her tablemates looked at all embarrassed.

When it was all over, Amy's team computed that they had earned forty-three points out of a possible fifty. They felt they had an excellent chance to finish in the money, maybe even win.

At 8:10 p.m., DJ Music Maker had finished grading the papers, and he began to go over the correct answers. Everything went as Amy's table had expected until question number 17, where, for the song title, the DJ said there were two correct alternate answers. "I'll accept either 'Will You Still Love Me Tomorrow'—which almost all of the tables wrote—or 'Will You Love Me Tomorrow,' which two tables wrote."

Three people at Amy's table breathed a very happy sigh of relief, but Amy, who was working feverously on her iPhone, was clearly unhappy and angry. She repeated several times, "This is not fair!"

Then she rose and spoke loudly, "I protest! Almost all of the tables were dead wrong! There are not two alternate titles. The title of the song is 'Will You Love Me Tomorrow.' I have, right here on YouTube, an image of the original Shirelles record, which proves that I am correct!"

All but two tables immediately began booing. There were shouts of things like, "Shut up and sit down," and "You got it right, lady. What are you complaining about?" As had happened when Amy had complained at previous trivias, Amy's tablemates noticeably lowered their heads and said nothing.

Then the DJ spoke, "It is widely accepted that 'Will You Still Love Me Tomorrow' is an alternate title. This is mentioned on Wikipedia; I just looked it up."

Amy was now in a rage. "It was widely accepted that the sun goes around the earth. You made a big thing about an answer being wrong if we put an extra word into the title. Goffin and King cowrote the song and gave it the title, 'Will You love Me

Tomorrow.' The Shirelles sang the song, and that's the title that appears on the record. Why are you violating your own rules, and only on this one song?"

The boos got louder, and the DJ announced, "As the judge, I am sticking to my original ruling. Miss, you may now sit down." Wild applause from the audience. Amy took her seat; her teammates still remained silent.

When the scores were announced, Amy's table came in second, with forty-three points. The winners had forty-five points. "So," Cathy pointed out, "we would have been second even if the DJ had scored question 17 properly."

Amy nodded. "Yes, it was all for nothing. And I knew all along that the DJ wouldn't change his original ruling. So I did it again, and I had promised Jerry I wouldn't."

"Forget it," said Eddie, "don't let it bother you." Jeremy gave Amy a big kiss. "They've started the dance music; let's go out there and dance." Knowing that Jeremy *never* wanted to dance and only did so as a result of her prodding, Amy smiled, nodded, and they proceeded onto the dance floor.

At 9:35 p.m., the foursome departed from Armando's. Amy and Jeremy arrived home at 10:30 p.m., and shortly thereafter, Amy began taking the necessary actions—with her husband's active participation—to satisfy her prolonged sexual tension due to Jeremy's extremely smart comments during dinner.

Afterward, Amy spent some time on her computer and verified what she already knew. "Jerry, there's no doubt whatsoever about it; I was right about the song title. People who throw in the word *still* in the title of that song—and, in particular, the Shirelles' number 1 hit version that the DJ played—are simply mistaken. I don't care how many people think so. It doesn't change the actual title. But that doesn't excuse what I did."

"Sweetheart, you shouldn't have done what you did, but the DJ was supposed to be the knowledgeable professional at this event. He made a bunch of strict rules, and then he was either unwilling to enforce them for this one particular song or he was terribly ignorant regarding a number 1 hit song that is world-famous. That is inexcusable. He bears most of the blame. And I'm not just trying to make you feel better."

Amy smiled. "Okay, I like your argument, and I second it. But I have to learn to control myself better."

Cathy and Eddie returned to their apartment, and as soon as they entered, they smiled at each other and then burst out laughing.

"Honey," said Eddie, between giggles, "don't they realize why we invite them, whenever possible, to join us at events like this?"

"You mean," chuckled Cathy, "you wonder if they realize that we look forward to Amy's righteous protests, and we find them hilarious! I'm pretty sure they have no idea. Do you think Jeremy also finds her funny, or is he upset with her antics?"

Her husband replied confidently, "I've known Jeremy since high school. I know from his face when he's upset. Trust me. He's not upset in the slightest when Amy goes off her rocker at trivia or Name That Tune or any similar event. He finds it amusing, but he won't let Amy know. And we won't either, right?

"Right," she replied. "Never!"

Monday, May 21, 2018

At age 47, Neil Starkman was the youngest current member of the board. Neil was the son of a well-known billionaire philanthropist and was involved in various charities. He had agreed to meet with Amy at 3:15 p.m. at his office in Garfield. Amy arrived fifteen minutes early and was told to take a seat in the reception room and wait.

At exactly 3:15 p.m., the inner door opened, and Neil greeted Amy and escorted his guest to his private office. He was six feet tall and in great shape. He immediately posed a question. "Amy, why did you agree to take on this case?"

"Well, that's my specialty at Spy4U, namely investigating hard-to-solve murder cases. Additionally, Christine Longley has been a valued client of ours in the past, and we want to provide as much assistance as possible to our past clients. Finally, I am personally enraged that someone may get away with murdering a dedicated educator working essentially for free for the benefit of a wonderful private academy and proposing changes she thought were necessary to save the school."

He nodded. "Amy, that is an excellent answer. I have researched you on the Internet, and I should have realized that you would give me a response to my question that was unchallengeable.

But the reality is that while I hate murderers and want them brought to justice, any success you achieve in identifying Mary's killer will likely be detrimental to the academy."

Amy shook her head. "Neil, now you've got me totally confused."

"Okay, I'll explain. Mary was a bully. And she was a big success at bullying, at least with regard to our board of trustees. She would mock viewpoints at variance with hers and insinuate that we were dumb, uninformed, improperly biased, or similar for expressing those views. Her tone of voice was that of authority and condescension. And we all folded to her. She almost always got her way on the board.

"If the committee, chaired by Mary, which came up with the proposal was anything like our board, then we can be confident that Mary bullied them all, and they caved. So the proposal was almost certainly entirely Mary's suggestions. And they are truly awful suggestions.

"When you eliminate all dance and theater, as well as reducing art and music to bare-bones status, you destroy the soul of a school. The academy would not be an exception. The intellectual diversity and the cultural diversity and richness of our student body would be destroyed. Everyone on the board knows that.

"And I'm sure Mary also knew that. But she got this bee in her bonnet that the only way to raise the scores and stop the academy from losing foundation support and closing down was to immediately enact her proposal. So she bullied, demeaned, insulted, and humiliated us into going along. Had she not been murdered, there is no doubt that at our meeting earlier this month, we would have unanimously voted to approve Mary's entire proposal."

Amy was dumbfounded. "Mary actually insulted the other board members?"

"Well, she was a bit more sophisticated than that. For example, she presented us with a blowup of a photo of a dance teacher at the academy showing some steps to two students. The teacher happened to be white, and the two students were African Americans. Mary said, 'Too many of us share the soft bigotry of lowered expectations. We figure it's okay if these two students have reading and math scores which are way below their potential if properly instructed. After all, see, they can dance well!' The obvious implication was that anyone who opposed her proposal was clearly a racist."

"Oh my god, oh my god! I had not heard anything like this from Polly and Peggy, the two board members I spoke to this past Saturday. May I quote you regarding Mary's behavior?"

He smiled. "Oh yes, you can quote me. And those two ladies on the board decided to pretend that Mary was just being enthusiastic. After all, she had done the research and had the facts, whereas they didn't. But as soon as Mary was murdered, they had the same view as I did. We had to delay the vote for a year and put together a new proposal that basically retains the arts. So their actions belie their expressed generosity toward Mary's conduct."

"Neil, why are you saying that if the murderer is identified and arrested, that would be bad for the academy? I would think it would be good for everyone involved."

"Amy, it seems to violate common sense, but given my background, I know how the people at the foundation think. Right now, Mary's murder has gone somewhat under the radar. The foundation is willing to give the board the extra time to try to find a substitute plan.

"However, if the murderer is found, the whole story becomes front-page news again. Everyone will be thinking about the fact that the scores on the basics had fallen at the academy and that Mary was killed to stop her proposal to raise the scores from being implemented. The strongest principle of the foundation is that the three basics are the bedrock of success in life. It is important to the foundation that they preserve their reputation in that regard. So I strongly suspect that if the arrest of the killer happens fairly soon, before an acceptable new proposal can be developed, the foundation would likely demand that Mary's proposal be immediately accepted, or they would sever their relationship.

"I can't prove I'm correct about this, but I know those people. If you solve the murder, I want to be wrong. But I have to let you know my feelings."

Amy nodded. "Of course, I want to know how you feel and what you believe to be true. And I greatly appreciate your candor, on everything. From what you say, disregarding Mary, the murder, and the foundation, I take it you would like to see an alternative proposal which preserves the arts."

He nodded vigorously. "Oh yes, if I was convinced that it included viable programs to raise the scores in the basics, I would gladly support such a revised proposal. And as things stand now, I would not be surprised to see such a proposal developed and approved unanimously by the board next May.

The board did exactly the right thing in postponing the vote and seeking alternatives."

The meeting ended, and Neil escorted his guest to the front door. Amy drove straight home and informed her husband that they were going out to eat at Clay's Steak House. "Get ready, I have some very interesting and unexpected information to present to you over dinner."

At Clay's, they settled in, and Amy kept her promise by relating the details of what Neil had told her. "Well, Jerry, what do you think of that?"

"Well, for one thing, I am very confident that Neil is mistaken in his belief that if the killer is identified and arrested, the foundation may go back on their previous approval of the one-year delay in the vote and of the search for a viable alternate proposal. I'm sure the foundation executives are honorable people, and that kind of response to the arrest of the killer would be thoroughly dishonorable."

His wife nodded. "I'm with you on that. I think Neil's reasoning is totally faulty. I hope I can solve the murder and prove him wrong."

"But, sweetheart, you're right that what Neil said about Mary's bullying and insulting behavior is unexpected and very surprising. And now we have a totally different but plausible interpretation of the words 'disgraceful actions' in the warning letter. If Mary was bullying and insulting to board members, then she was likely to have acted similarly toward other people having no connection to the academy. We may have been on the wrong track here all along."

Amy was not convinced. "Maybe, but do you think people whom Mary bullied and insulted during her everyday life would actually murder her? Remember, this was a planned murder, not a spur-of-the-moment rage killing."

He smiled. "Would bullied people from her everyday life actually murder her? No, for the vast majority, but you only need one bullied person."

She nodded. "Jerry, you do have a point."

"Sweetheart, do you think maybe Neil was exaggerating?"

"Maybe, but he did provide one specific disgusting, insulting quote from Mary. Of course, he may not have recalled it precisely, word for word, but what he said was likely very close to the real thing." Amy gave her husband the quote regarding the dance teacher and the students.

Jeremy nodded. "You're right. I guess Neil was probably not exaggerating. Now you have to go find the people, if any, that Mary badly bullied and insulted. They are all suspects."

His wife smiled. "Yeah, swell. My obvious action right now is to phone Christine." She punched in the number and put on the speaker.

"Hello, Christine, this is Amy. I have a question for you which is not related solely to the academy. It's been asserted by a board member that Mary has frequently been insulting and a bully when dealing with people she may disagree with. Have you ever seen or been informed about this kind of behavior by Mary in any circumstance whatsoever?"

"Sorry, Amy, but I never saw her acting that way or heard about that kind of behavior. Are you sure this bullying story is on the up-and-up? I find it very hard to believe."

"I do too, but I've got to check it out." After a bit of small talk, Amy got off the phone. "So, Jerry, Christine knows nothing about any bullying by Mary."

"Sweetheart, that would not be so surprising. Just like not telling Christine about the two warning letters, Mary didn't want to upset her old friend with unpleasant things regarding her relationships with some other residents of the township."

Amy nodded. "That does make sense. But I wish Christine could have provided some names of people bullied by Mary—if there actually are any."

"I'll bet Mary's problems with some of her neighbors in Teaneck were related to Mary insulting and bullying them."

"Jerry, I'll bet you're right. Christine said Mary never told her what was the problem she had with her neighbors. So it could easily have involved bullying. I've got to check that out."

"Sweetheart, you can't be suggesting that someone living in Teaneck whom she bullied ten years ago finally decided to murder her this past April."

"Of course not, but maybe I can find out the details of what was the nature of her bullying. Then maybe I can determine whom she may have been bullying recently in Ferman Township. Right now, I have almost nothing to go on. I'm looking for anything that might help."

"Who's next on your list of interviews?"

"Matthew Birch, the fourth and final current board member. I'm meeting him tomorrow at twelve thirty for lunch, and guess where?"

He laughed. "How about the Ferman Country Diner?"

"Good guess! I'll see if he agrees that Mary was a big bully."

Tuesday, May 22, 2018

Matthew Birch was sixty years old, and with his thin face and narrow mustache, Amy decided that he reminded her of Charlie Chaplin. She knew he was a professor of education at a local college. They shook hands and ordered their drinks and meals. Then Matthew cautioned her regarding his usefulness with regard to the investigation.

"Amy, I'm the newest member of the board; I just started on February first. I'm still very much in the learning mode. When Mary presented her committee's proposal, I did not feel capable of making too many informed comments to contribute to the discussion. I listened carefully and eventually agreed with everyone else that the proposals should be approved by the board at their meeting in early May.

"Then on April 14, Mary was shot and killed. The more experienced members of the board realized at that point that they had nearly totally relied on Mary in deciding to approve the proposal. I fully understood their feeling that a year of further study and review could possibly reveal an alternative that retains more of the arts programs that we were going to eliminate or substantially reduce.

"As I said, I was basically still a listener. And I decided that what I heard at that point made good sense, provided that the foundation people went along with the one-year delay. They did, indeed, agree, so we voted unanimously to do the additional research and defer the vote until May 2019.

"I am very grateful to the Ferman PD for providing us with extra protection, but from what I hear, they're not making much progress on the murder case. I'm hoping you can pull off a miracle and identify the killer. I wish I could help you, but frankly I don't see how."

Amy smiled. "Matthew, I have discovered, during my time in the detective business, that people like you can think that what you're saying will not be helpful and then some small, seemingly useless piece of information that you provide turns out to be critical in solving the case.

"In any case, do you agree with Neil, who is your colleague on the board, that Mary's behavior toward the board members while discussing her proposal was bullying and insulting?"

He shook his head. "I can understand how Neil—and maybe other board members—might have felt that way. But I don't think Mary intended to be bullying or insulting. She was just trying to be a strong and enthusiastic advocate for her proposal, which she fully believed was necessary to save the academy.

"I got to know Mary during the brief period when she and I were on the board together; for some reason, we enjoyed talking to each other. She was truly a caring person. And she was a hero, too—well, I guess I should call her a heroine. Very few people are aware of this, but some years ago, she risked her own life to save the life of a stranger she had never previously met."

"Oh my god, Matthew, can you provide some details?"

"I'll tell you what Mary told me. It was while she was still living in Teaneck. She drove to Noble Grove—about twenty miles to the west—to visit a friend. During her time there, she decided to walk from where she parked the car to a nearby park. So there she was, walking down the street—"

"I have to ask you this," interrupted Amy, with a big smile on her face. "Was she shuffling her feet and singing 'do wah diddy?' Of course, I realize she might not have mentioned any of those details."

He was totally bewildered. "What? Am I missing something?"

"Oh, sorry, Matthew, my mind was somewhere else. Please continue."

"Okay, she saw this man only a few feet away, walking across a two-way street in the middle of the block while working on his iPhone and not realizing that a car was coming at him. The car didn't look like it was slowing down. Mary didn't pause to decide what to do. She ran out and pushed the man forward and away from the car's path, also barely managing to avoid the car herself. The car never stopped.

"The man—she told me his first name was Jasper and she couldn't recall his last name—took down Mary's name and address and said he would mail a thousand-dollar check to charity and tell them the donation was in her honor. He also said he hated his relatives and would make Mary the sole beneficiary of his will. She told him not to do that; the charitable donation would be more than enough of a thank-you."

Amy laughed. "That's because Mary was filthy rich through her husband's inherited money. If anyone wants to put me in their will, I say, 'You go, guy!'"

Now Matthew laughed, then he continued, "Also, Mary volunteered, one day per week, to help prepare and serve meals for the needy. So to summarize, she was a wonderful, caring person who occasionally got somewhat carried away with her enthusiasm."

Amy flashed a big smile. Now she understood. "Matthew, are you married?"

"No, I've been divorced since 2008."

"In that case, based on what you've told me, I'm pretty sure Mary was after you. Of course, I could be wrong, but you had only known her for a brief period of time, and she was telling you all this stuff that I doubt she told anyone else. Do you agree? Did you pick up that vibe?"

He nodded. "Amy, I never picked up on it, but now that you're saying it, I realize you're probably right. Now I'm kicking myself; I'm truly a jerk. If I had realized it, I definitely would have let Mary know I was also interested."

"Did Mary ever mention some sort of dispute she may have had with anyone, such as a neighbor or a storekeeper, for example?"

He checked for some information on his iPhone. "Every member of the board had to provide the contact information for their attorney, in case a legal issue might arise. Mary submitted the information for Aaron Ryman. His office is here in Ferman Township. You probably should contact him to answer your question. I personally don't know of any disputes. Mary and I almost always talked about positive things."

Amy smiled. "Matthew, contrary to your feeling that you could not be of assistance to my investigation, my meeting with you may well turn out to be the most helpful of all four of my meetings with the board members."

"Wow, Amy, I find that quite hard to believe, but I certainly hope that I helped!"

After they finished their lunch, Amy drove to Spy4U, and at 3:15 p.m., she phoned her husband with the update. "So, Jerry, what do you think?"

"Sweetheart, this is easy. Matthew had a thing for Mary—although he never let Mary know—so he found a generous interpretation for Mary's bullying and insults, calling them excess enthusiasm. And I'm sure that as Mary had a thing for Matthew, and also as Matthew had just recently joined the board, she did not direct any of her nastiness toward Matthew, just toward the other three."

"Yes, I agree with you on that, but what about the will?"

Her husband was confused. "Okay, you tell me; what about the will? Do you mean Jasper's will?"

Yes, Jerry, of course I mean Jasper's will. That's the only will that came up in the conversation. Don't you see how it could possibly be a motive for Mary's murder?"

"No, I don't."

"Well, my other phone is ringing; let me get off. Think about it; I'll lay out the whole thing for you, if necessary, when I get home."

The other caller turned out to be Cathy. "Amy, ever since the Name That Tune event, I've been thinking about what Jeremy said about extra police protection. Even though Barbara, the murder victim, did not tell the police about the warning letters, any potential murderer would assume that Barbara would, indeed, tell the police, and then Barbara would likely be provided with extra protection."

Amy was about to ask Cathy, "Who the hell is Barbara?" But then, just in time, she realized that Barbara was the name she had used instead of Mary when discussing the case with Cathy and Eddie.

Cathy continued, "So someone contemplating murder would never send such letters, whether or not the intention was diversion from the true motive. Therefore, I think Jeremy is wrong. The letters were not sent as a diversion. The letter writer probably was angry about the school proposal and hoped the threats in the letters would cause Barbara to withdraw or change the proposal. As Jeremy pointed out, that hope was unrealistic, but the letter writer did not realize it.

"However, the letter writer never planned, under any circumstances, to actually murder Barbara. The killer was a different person who had no knowledge of or connection to the letters.

The fact that the letters came shortly before the murder was just a coincidence."

Amy was impressed. "Cathy, you make a very logical argument. I'll present it to Jerry this evening and see how he responds."

And that's what she did after dinner. "So has Cathy demolished your diversion theory?"

Jeremy smiled. "Cathy has demolished my diversion theory only if she has also demolished your theory that the letter sender was angry about Mary's proposal. You would then have to agree the whole letter thing was just a big coincidence, totally unrelated to the murder."

Amy stroked her husband on the cheek. "Poor boy, you haven't thought about it carefully enough. My theory is a two-step theory, while yours has only one step."

"Sweetheart, what the heck are you talking about?"

"Your theory has the killer knowing from the start that she would murder Mary and sending the letters to create a diversion as a part of her original plan. My theory has two steps, occurring at two widely separated times. The first step, likely beginning in March, was when the eventual killer sent the first and then in early April, the second letter. At that point, she had not yet decided to kill Mary—and probably hadn't even thought about killing her. She just wanted to pressure Mary into changing her proposal." Amy continued stroking Jeremy's cheek.

"The second step didn't occur until mid-April, when she realized Mary was standing firm on her proposal. Now she became even more enraged, at a whole new level, where she was willing to kill Mary. It was too late to worry about the police protection, as the threatening letters could not now be rescinded. She had previously, for some reason, procured a stolen gun with a silencer. Or possibly she was able to quickly acquire the gun. She used it to murder Mary." Amy stopped stroking and produced a gotcha smile.

"Sweetheart, as you have said, we should not overthink this and assume the murderer was smart and sophisticated. This was likely the first time she ever did something like this. She might have sent the letters as a diversion without even considering that there might be added police protection for Mary."

Amy nodded. "Yes, Jerry, I'll admit you have a point. And even smart people do dumb things, which they don't realize were mistakes until much later. Now have you figured out how Jasper's will could provide a motive for Mary's murder?"

Jeremy shook his head. "No, I've been thinking about it, but I have no idea."

"Okay, let's say Jasper is single and has three living relatives, whom he hates. So he made Mary his sole beneficiary and announced it to his relatives. Therefore, if Jasper dies before Mary, Mary inherits everything. But if Jasper dies after Mary, his relatives may inherit.

"Now, of course, Jasper could have stated in his will that if Mary cannot inherit, the money goes to charity or to a friend. So the relatives would not be sure whether they would inherit. But pretend Jasper is now very ill or very old. One of the relatives might decide to kill Mary now, prior to Jasper's death, to preserve their chance to inherit.

"Therefore, we have to locate Jasper, find out who are his relatives, and find out the specifics of his will, if possible. Then if the relatives still qualify as suspects, we can try to determine their whereabouts on April 14, the day Mary was murdered."

Jeremy was not convinced. "Sweetheart, that's quite a stretch, isn't it? After all, Mary saved Jasper over a decade ago. That's when he would have put Mary into his will. And no one tried to kill Mary until now. I find that hard to believe."

"Jerry, I'm guessing that there has recently been some sort of change in Jasper's health which makes his death likely in the near future and which has focused his relatives' attention on the provisions of his will.

"Of course, I could be way off base on this whole thing. We don't know that Jasper actually made Mary the sole beneficiary—or even any kind of beneficiary—of his will. We don't know whether Jaspar is a very old man and/or a very sick man. But there's only one way we can know what's going on, and that's by doing some investigating. Luckily there are people at Spy4U who can work on this for me.

"And I also have to speak to Aaron Ryman, who Matthew said Mary listed as her attorney. Matthew felt—and I agree—that Aaron would likely be the one to know if Mary had an issue with neighbors or other people in Ferman Township.

"Again, it's possible that Mary's bullying, while residing in the township, was only done to board members. But I doubt it. And regardless, I want to find out what kind of dispute she had with her neighbors in Teaneck."

"So, sweetheart, who's next on your list of interviews?"

"I think I'll contact Anna Morgenson for an appointment. She's the school principal at Ferman Academy. Anna can tell me about what she believes are the viable alternatives, if any, to Mary's proposal. Of course, due to her position, she strongly wants to preserve jobs and programs, but she certainly does not want the school to have to close down."

Her husband smiled. "There's basically only one question I'd be anxious to ask if I were interviewing Anna. The rest are just filler material."

"Okay, Jerry, I'll bite. What's the question?"

"Anna, have you ever visited the Adriatic region of Europe, and if so, did you purchase one or more pairs of shoes while you were there?" This resulted in both of them erupting in laughter. When they calmed down, Amy had a question.

"So you think Anna is a suspect?"

"Well, sweetheart, I assume she was very much opposed to Mary's proposal. Also, there's a chance she bought a pair of lady's shoes for someone else, and we'd want to know who was that other lady. Or, of course, someone else was over there and bought the shoes for Anna. Or maybe the shoes actually can be purchased somewhere on the Internet."

She smiled. "I guess you've covered all the possibilities. But you know, Jerry, you're right. Anna is a prime suspect, as are, of course, all the female teachers of subjects in danger of being eliminated or curtailed. I don't know why I wasn't thinking about Anna in that way. That's very smart of you, and you know what that does to me."

Jerry knew, and he realized that the current discussion was over, at least for the next hour and a half.

Thursday, May 24, 2018

The Ferman Academy was a modern-looking four-story building with an exterior of shiny metal and lots of glass. Definitely not what Amy had expected. It was on an elevated location with a nice view of the township below.

The corner office of the principal was on the fourth floor, so Anna had the best possible view. At 11:15 a.m., they shook hands and agreed to use first names. The principal was fifty-seven years old, five foot six, and a bit plump. She had a kind-looking face with an appealing smile. Amy got the ball rolling.

"Anna, I think everyone agrees that Mary supported her proposal because she felt that it was the best way to get the scores up sufficiently in the basics and stop the academy from having to shut down. How did you respond to that?"

"Amy, I'm going to surprise you. Mary was correct. Her proposal provided the best chance of sufficiently raising the scores in the basics.

"Her plan was to eliminate the vast majority of our arts classes and substitute double periods of the courses in English and mathematics for three of the five days per week This means that on those three days, the classes would last twice as long compared to now. There would also be a separate writing class, whereas we currently incorporate that into our English classes. All those classes would be required of all our students.

"Additional specialists would be hired to essentially prep the students for the relevant standardized examinations. And of course, many teachers in the arts would be let go, and their courses would be abolished.

"Please understand that we currently have excellent teachers of English and mathematics. And Mary never suggested otherwise. Those teachers would remain; the prep specialists would be co-instructors for those classes.

"I have conceded that this proposal gave the academy the best chance of sufficiently raising the scores. So why did I strongly oppose Mary's proposal? Because we would be throwing the baby out with the bathwater. We would be left with a school that fails to provide a well-rounded education. It would fail to address the student's whole mental and human aspects. I would never send my child to such a school, nor would most of the parents of the type of students we are looking for.

"I do support an alternative which has a good chance of raising the scores, although admittedly not as good a chance as Mary's proposal. We can hire specialists to prepare effective study programs in the basics for students to accomplish online at home. We can also offer summer prep classes online.

"The online work would not be mandatory, but the students would understand that diligently studying the online material would likely improve their grades in the academy's English and math classes and increase their chances of admission to the college of their choice. The extra costs of running the online programs would be manageable.

"As it stands now, that's my alternative. There may also be other reasonable alternative proposals, and I may also decide to incorporate some of their ideas into my alternative. I hope the board analyzes all such proposals and settles on one of them—or possibly a combination of two or more proposals. I am optimistic that next May, the board will approve an appropriate nondraconian alternative to Mary's proposal.

"You have requested a full list of faculty members at the academy, including their subjects taught, plus a list of administrators. Here it is." She handed a sheet of paper to Amy. "However, I have informed these people that they can choose to meet with you or choose to decline to meet with you. No pressure and no penalties."

Amy nodded. "I completely understand. May I ask if you had met with Mary, and if so, did she ever speak to you—or to anyone else, to the best of your knowledge—in a bullying or insulting manner?"

"Yes, I met with Mary several times. She was always friendly and civil, both to me and to everyone else I heard her speaking to. Furthermore, no one ever told me she was insulting or acting like a bully. My issue with Mary was solely regarding what changes should be made at the academy. And to answer your next question, it is inconceivable to me that any member of the faculty or administration at the academy would send a threatening letter to Mary, let alone murder her."

Amy smiled. "To be honest, that was not gonna be my next question; in fact, I was desperately trying to think of a good question to ask." That comment resulted in hearty laughter from the principal. When she calmed down, she summed up her feelings.

"You know, Amy, I really like you. You don't fit the mold of a detective. But I'm very confident that you won't find the killer if you concentrate on the staff working at the academy. However, I guess I can't vouch for the sanity of each parent who has a child enrolled in the academy. So one of those parents theoretically could have murdered Mary; I won't deny that, although I doubt it. Anyhow, good luck; I certainly hope you can nail the killer."

Shortly thereafter, Amy departed the academy and drove to her Spy4U office. She stopped at Subway along the way to buy a six-inch double-meat roast beef sub for lunch, which she consumed at her desk. Then she phoned her husband and related her interview with Anna. "So, Jerry, what do you think?"

"No surprises whatsoever, unless you thought Mary would have bullied the principal. Also, I would be very skeptical that any at-home online study program would significantly raise scores in the basics. Frankly, I'm beginning to think Mary was right all along. If the goal is to raise scores sufficiently to prevent the academy from being shut down, Mary's proposal should probably be adopted."

"Well, the principal suggested that there may be other alternative proposals which may be very different in their approach from the alternative she described to me."

Jeremy was not impressed. "As I see it, all the alternatives are likely to be primarily aimed at preserving the arts classes. Mary's proposal, on the other hand, was entirely aimed at raising scores in the basics and thereby keeping the academy open for business."

"You may be right. Anyhow, as I previously said, determining the best course of action is way above my pay grade."

"Sweetheart, do you agree with Anna that the killer might be a parent but it's extremely unlikely that an academy employee murdered Mary?"

Amy laughed. "No, of course, I do not agree with that. Anna is, understandably, loyal to her staff. As you had mentioned, nothing she said was surprising."

At this point in the conversation, there was a knock on Amy's office door. It was Chester. As she motioned to her boss to take a seat, Amy told Jeremy that she had to get off the phone. "So, Mr. Murray, what brings you to this neck of the woods?"

"Amy, how are things going with the Mary Rackner murder case?"

"Well, I've done some interviews, and I'm learning some interesting information that may or may not eventually turn out to be useful. But so far, no breakthroughs, and as I told Jerry, I'm rather pessimistic."

He nodded. "As you know, it's still very early. Anyhow, Spy4U has recently become a magnet for our previous clients. First, Christine and now Richard Smith. He's an investment fund manager.

"Richard likes to retain us to thoroughly check out his new girl-friends—or potential new girlfriends. I think we're up to five women so far, and Richard is still a bachelor, so the total may end up much higher before he finally finds a sufficiently compatible woman for whom we can provide a clean bill of health."

"How old is Richard?" inquired Amy.

"Thirty-six, as I recall. He lives in Flushing, Queens."

Amy smiled. "Maybe you should try to fix him up with the nanny."

She proceeded to laugh at her own joke as Chester continued, "Richard thinks one of his acquaintances took down his credit card number and used it to make political contributions. Can you meet with him in my office tomorrow at ten in the morning? I told him you're the one—if there's anyone, it's you—to try to identify the culprit for him. He knows it'll be your decision as to whether to take a shot at it, and he knows that due to your murder investigation, you can only spare at most three days on his case, if you accept it."

"Political contributions?" Again, Amy started laughing. "Someone used his card number to make political contributions? Richard's gotta be kidding!"

"Well, Amy, that's what he told me. If you want more details—and I'm sure you do—you'll have to wait till you see him tomorrow morning."

"Okay, Mr. Murray, I certainly am intrigued. I'll see you and Richard at ten in the morning tomorrow in your office." Chester exited, and Amy again phoned her husband and explained what had transpired after she had to hang up. "Political contributions? Jerry, can you believe that?"

"Sweetheart, that might make sense if the culprit is a political junkie, like you!"

"Yeah, Jerry, you do have a point. Now I'm really looking forward to meeting with Richard tomorrow and learning all the details."

Friday, May 25, 2018

The two men were already seated in Chester's office when Amy entered and decided that Richard Smith was a real hunk. Six foot two—at least, that's how Chester had described Richard to her earlier that morning—and clearly in great physical shape, with a neat mustache that augmented his sexy look. Amy also noted that Richard was clearly giving her the once-over. He eyed her—up and down—much longer than would ever be considered appropriate. Finally, he rose—confirming his height—and shook Amy's hand; then they both took their seats. They agreed to use first names, and Richard began his presentation.

"I am a member of the Flushing Non-Partisan Political Club. The members are men and women who are very interested in politics and enjoy friendly discussion and debate. We have social activities, as well as special occasions when we invite speakers. The club has been a great success. No bitterness, no antagonism, and many friendships have been created. We also learn a lot. The club generally meets in a room at the local Elks Club. Sometimes we host parties at our own homes.

"I would not say I've gained friends at the club, but rather, a decent number of very cordial acquaintances, almost all of them men—dammit!" Everyone laughed. "Actually, that's no surprise, as the large majority of the club members are men.

Well, I guess I can call these acquaintances friends if I use the term loosely, but they're not close friends if you know what I mean. And for some reason, although there are Republicans and independents in the club, these friends are all Democrats, like me." Again, laughter all around.

"On Saturday, May 12, I attended an event, from one thirty to four in the afternoon, run by a different but similar organization. It was held in the banquet room of a local restaurant. There were drinks and snacks, and some candidates for local office were invited to make brief presentations and then socialize with us. Four of my friends from our club—all of them men—also attended. As with our club, there were people there from both parties, as well as independents. People from all over Queens attended. The big difference was that roughly half the attendees were women. I got two ladies' phone numbers, and I've already had a rather productive date with one of them, if you know what I mean." More laughs.

"Shortly after I arrived, I realized that I had to provide my travel agent with my Visa credit card number prior to the three o'clock deadline to pay for a cruise I had booked. For some reason, I wasn't getting cellular phone service at that location, but luckily, there was a landline phone on a small table. I took out my credit card, phoned my agent, and gave her my card number. What I didn't realize was that after giving the card number, I was distracted, placed my Visa card on the small table, and left it there after I had finished the phone call.

"About an hour later, I realized what had happened, so I walked back to the table, and there was my credit card, still sitting there. I put the card into my wallet and congratulated myself on my good luck.

"Three days ago, on this past Tuesday, I received a letter from Romney-for-Senate thanking me for my two-hundred-dollar contribution, charged to my Visa credit card. The problem was that I had not contributed to Mitt Romney, nor to any other candidate.

"I contacted the Visa people, and they informed me that three separate political contributions had been made using my Visa card in the days shortly after I had left my card on the table. In addition to Romney-for-Senate in Utah, there were contributions to Angus King's Senate reelection campaign in Maine and Nancy Pelosi's House reelection campaign in California. All contributions were two hundred dollars.

"There had been no other fraudulent use of the card. But, of course, at that point, I immediately had them cancel my Visa card. They're sending me a new card with a new number.

"I checked with the three candidates' campaigns. When people phone them to make contributions, in addition to all the credit card information, they obtain the donor's name and address. They also ask for an email, but that's optional. And the campaigns all did, indeed, have my correct name and address, while an email had not been provided. This virtually guarantees that one of my four friends saw my card on the table, took down my card information, and then put the card back on the table. They are the only four people there who would know my address.

"I told my four friends about my Visa card being left on the table and then being used fraudulently. I also told them I was planning to hire a detective to try to get to the bottom of it. I lied and told them I figured that some stranger at the event must have taken down my card information, and I wanted my friends to meet with the detective to provide any observations they might recall from the event that might conceivably help. They all acted very sympathetic and said they'd be happy to help me out, although they all expressed doubts that they could contribute much, if anything."

Amy had a question. "Richard, did you provide your friends with the names of the candidates to whom contributions were made with your card?"

"No, I just said my card was used to make political contributions. By the way, they are all willing to meet with you, if you wish, at Starbucks on Northern Boulevard in Flushing—or at any other restaurant in that area—this Saturday or Sunday afternoon."

Now Richard flashed a big smile. "Amy, I have to ask you the most important question of all. Are you married or otherwise spoken for? You are a beautiful, smart, and—at least for me—a very exciting woman. And I would not have to hire Spy4U to check you out. Sorry, Chester, but I can't help myself!"

Chester laughed and looked at Amy, who was smiling. "Richard, I really appreciate your compliments, but I'm very happily married."

Richard looked very depressed as Amy continued, "Okay, let's set up all four interviews for this Sunday afternoon at Starbucks. My husband assists me with my cases, so he would also attend. If you agree to that, I'll accept the case, with the understanding that I can only spare a couple of days and that solving something like this is always a long shot."

Still looking morose, he responded, "Yes, I fully understand. I'll set up the four interviews at Starbucks for Sunday. And I'll tell them to use first names."

Amy exited Chester's office to allow the men to finalize all the details. At three in the afternoon, Richard got back to Amy with the address of the Starbucks, the names of his friends, and the times of the four Sunday interviews.

When Amy got home, she provided her husband with all the details of Richard's presentation and noted the political affiliations of the three candidates who received the $200 contributions. "I asked for the interviews to be on Sunday so as not to interfere with your Saturday tennis match. What's your take on all this?"

Jeremy nodded. "Thanks for doing it on Sunday. My first reaction is that if one of Richard's Democrat friends is the culprit, why did that friend contribute money to an independent and to a Republican?"

She stroked his cheek. "Poor boy, you simply don't understand politics. Utah is a solid-red Republican state. Whoever wins the Republican Senate primary in June will almost surely be elected to the Senate in November. So all sophisticated Democrats—like me and the credit card culprit—want the most moderate Republican candidate to win the Republican primary. In this case, that's Mitt Romney." She continued stroking.

"Now in Maine, it's a bit of a different story. The incumbent, Angus King, is officially an independent, as is Senator Bernie Sanders from Vermont. But just like Sanders, King almost always votes with the Democrats in the Senate. Now the Democrats will have a Senate candidate—not King—on the ballot in November, but that candidate has no chance to win. The only two candidates who can win are King and the Republican.

"And it looks like Maine will be introducing ranked-choice voting this year. This means there will be a so-called instant runoff if no candidate receives over 50 percent of the initial vote. There may be some voter confusion on this, so again, sophisticated Democrats will contribute to the King campaign to help get out as large an initial vote for him as possible."

She stopped stroking and continued, "It's logical that most of the members of the political groups that Richard is talking about would be sophisticated, knowledgeable people and would know all about Romney's and King's situations. And they would also know that Nancy Pelosi, who is a sure winner in her San Francisco congressional district, uses a lot of her campaign money to help other Democrat candidates—and she knows exactly which ones will benefit most from her help.

"So for any of Richard's four Democrat friends to select those three candidates for contributions would be perfectly understandable. And that would also be true for any other Democrat at the event."

Jeremy smiled. "Thanks for the political analysis. Richard said he knows the culprit is one of his four friends because only those four knew his address. But aren't there websites where you put in someone's name and town and their address comes up?"

"Yes, but do you have any idea how many Richard Smiths live in Flushing, let alone all of Queens? That's a very common name. If his name was Angkor Zirconium, you may indeed have made a good point." Laughter from the both of them. "Also, I have found that those sites are often far from accurate and frequently not updated for recent changes in address."

"Sweetheart, what you just said reinforces my opinion that the friend who is the culprit is the opposite of sophisticated. He's basically a fool. He could have used Richard's Visa card number to make all sorts of online and phone purchases where the buyer does not have to provide an address. By providing Richard's address, he limits the suspects to just Richard's four friends, rather than all the men at the event. I said all the men because I'll assume a woman would not phone a campaign and pretend to be Richard, although I'm not even sure of that, come to think of it.

"Also, he might have gotten away with making other purchases with the card for a lot longer period of time before Richard got wise. With the political contributions, Richard was quickly alerted."

Amy shook her head. "I don't agree. Say the culprit buys an item on the phone or online and uses Richard's card number. Where and to whom does he have the item delivered? By providing this information, the culprit is directly incriminating himself. So using Richard's card for a political contribution in Richard's name was—in that sense—absolutely brilliant.

"The culprit undoubtedly did not realize that the Romney campaign would mail Richard a thank-you note. If that had not occurred, and if Richard did not carefully check his Visa card statements, he might never have realized that the three contributions were charged to his account. And maybe, at some point in the future, the culprit would use Richard's card number to make additional political campaign contributions.

"So the culprit was sophisticated, not only politically but also criminally. Richard clearly has high-class friends, again using that term loosely, as he said." Amy laughed at her joke; her husband just smiled.

"Sweetheart, isn't it unusual for a restaurant to have a landline phone at a small table in its banquet room?"

She nodded. "Yes, but if they know that there is some sort of issue with cellular service at their location, they may put in the phone for the convenience of their banquet room guests."

"So as usual, I presume you want me to sit there quietly as you interview the suspects at Starbucks, right?"

"Yes, that's right. If you want to say something during an interview, whisper it in my ear, and I'll decide if it's appropriate for you to say it to the suspect. Of course, they don't know that they're suspects; Richard told them I need their help in trying to solve the case.

"After each interview, I'll ask you for your impressions. However, as usual, I won't make any judgements until all the interviews have finished. They begin at one thirty and then every half hour, with the last interview scheduled for three o'clock. Richard is scheduled to show up at three thirty to see how things went. And don't stuff yourself with pastries. It's okay to have one, but no more."

Jeremy smiled. "Don't get upset, but I think that to fully appreciate the interviews and to maintain silence, I'll need two pastries. Probably a cinnamon coffee cake and a double chocolate brownie. Otherwise, I may not be able to control myself, and I may start speaking uncontrollably during the interviews." He burst into hysterical laughter, and Amy knew it would be useless to debate this topic.

"Sweetheart, if you can identify the culprit, what do you think Richard would then do?"

"I doubt he'll do anything. I figure he just wants to know who did it so that he can appropriately adjust how he deals with that person. Based on his job and his behavior, he seems like a pretty wealthy guy to me. It's not the money he's worried about. Besides, the Visa people undoubtedly refunded all the fraudulent contribution money back to Richard. And he canceled the card, so the culprit can't strike again.

"Also, I have an idea or two on how to maybe identify the culprit. But I seriously doubt I have any chance whatsoever to uncover anything remotely qualifying as probable cause for an arrest. And believe me, I'll consider myself lucky if any of my ideas actually work and I can tell Richard which friend of his used his card number."

"Why would a friend—or anyone for that matter—use Richard's card number to make a political donation in Richard's name? The culprit gets no money whatsoever out of this transaction and gets no other benefit that I can see."

Amy was contemplative for several seconds, then she responded, "The best explanation I can see is that the culprit—who is overwhelmingly likely to be one of the four friends—actually has some sort of grudge against Richard and thought that this was a way to get back at him. Of course, this could be part of some sort of practical joke being pulled on Richard, but I think the joker or jokers would have come clean by this point."

Jeremy shook his head. "But as I just pointed out, Richard wasn't hurt at all by this stunt, except for the hassle of canceling his Visa card and getting a new one. So the friend didn't get anything that could reasonably be called revenge for Richard's real or perceived offense against him."

Amy nodded. "You have a good point. Of course, as long as the aggrieved friend is now satisfied, that's all that counts."

Her husband had another idea. "What if the friend is some sort of psycho and does these kinds of things because he has an uncontrollable urge to do so and it turns him on?"

She smiled. "Yeah, that's also a possibility. We'll get a good look at all four of them on Sunday, and maybe we'll decide that one—or more—of them is indeed nuts." They both laughed.

Sunday, May 27, 2018

Jeremy was about halfway through his double-chocolate brownie when the first friend, Martin Langston, arrived at Starbucks at one o'clock on the dot. He observed Amy wearing a red scarf, which Richard had told his friends she'd be wearing to make her easy to identify. So he immediately approached Amy and Jeremy, joining them at their table.

Martin was in his early forties and very well dressed, wearing a jacket and tie. They exchanged a few pleasantries, and then Amy began the interview. "So, Martin, what do you do for a living?"

"I'm an independent insurance agent, and I sell a wide variety of insurance products. But my true love is politics. I'm a real political junkie. And I guess that's true of the majority of members in the Flushing Non-Partisan Political Club."

Amy nodded. "Yeah, I think you're probably right about most of the club members. Richard hired me because at the May 12 event, he accidentally left his Visa card on a table, next to the phone, and someone copied down the card number. That person left the card there and then, later on, used the card number to make three $200 donations, in Richard's name, to the House or Senate campaigns of Romney, King, and Pelosi. I'm asking everyone if they can provide any observations from that May

12 event—no matter how minor—as even the smallest piece of information might possibly help me identify the culprit."

"Amy, I checked you out on the web. You like to solve murders, right?"

She smiled. "Well, I like solving murders much more than when I fail to solve them." Laughter all around.

"So why did you accept this ridiculous case?"

"Martin, the answer to that must be obvious to you; I accepted this case because Richard is paying me good money to do the investigation. Why do you say it's a ridiculous case?"

"I'll tell you why. Richard must have received a full refund of the fraudulent campaign donations, right?"

She nodded. "Right, as I understand it."

"Richard canceled the Visa card, so nobody can use that number to make any more purchases, right?"

"Right."

"So Richard has lost zero dollars, and now he has chosen to pay you big bucks to take on this case. That's absolutely ridiculous, and Richard must be crazy! What am I missing?"

"Martin, what you're missing is that Richard is not thinking about the money. He strongly believes that the culprit should not be allowed to get away with committing fraud—at least not without a fight."

He nodded. "I guess I should respect that. Okay, Amy, how can I help you?"

"Just tell me anything you recall about the event on May 12."

"Unfortunately, I remember very little. But whoever used the card would have done a lot better to make their donation to a Democrat in a purple district who can really use the money, as opposed to Pelosi, who is a sure winner in November and definitely does not need the money. Don't even ask me why someone who would donate to Pelosi would also donate to Romney.

"Anyhow, I definitely recall seeing the phone on a table in the back of the hall, which made sense, as my cell phone had no service in that room. I also remember seeing several guests—but not Richard—using the phone. I never noticed a credit card on the table."

"Do you know the name of anyone you saw using that phone, or can you describe them?"

"No, I can't, sorry. Thinking about the candidates who received the contributions, I wonder if someone may be playing some kind of big joke on Richard. Have you considered that?"

Amy nodded. "As I matter of fact, yes. I was discussing that possibility with my husband just this past Friday. Right, Jerry?"

Jeremy realized that this was an exception to Amy's "keep your mouth shut" rule, so he smiled and responded, "Yes, that's true."

The interview ended, and Amy smiled at her husband. "Okay, Jerry, that was kinda fun. What are your observations?"

"Well, first of all, Martin may view himself as a political junkie, but he is not very sophisticated, politically speaking. He hadn't thought of the reasons you gave me why a Democrat would contribute to the Pelosi and Romney campaigns."

She nodded. "You're sure as hell right about that. These club members may not be as politically sophisticated as I had thought."

"Also, he reinforced a good point which we had previously discussed. Who pays big bucks to Spy4U to find out which friend—to use the term very loosely—made a fraudulent use of his card when he has been totally reimbursed by Visa and therefore has sustained no loss whatsoever? Why not save your money and simply not trust any of those four, if a trust situation would ever even arise in the future?"

Amy smiled. "I guess the answer is that only a very rich guy does that. And Richard is obviously very rich. He also pays us to check out every woman with whom he has or might have a relationship. So it looks like money is no issue for him whatsoever. In that situation, why not try to identify the culprit?"

At 1:55 p.m., Roger Pender shook hands with Amy and Jeremy and joined them at the table. He was in his late thirties, appeared quite overweight, and was wearing a New York Mets sweatshirt. Amy started with some humor. "So, Roger, what position do you play for the Mets?"

He laughed. "Well, as you could have guessed, I do not play for the Mets, but I have done some computer work for them. I'm an IT specialist. And my hobby is politics."

"Okay, Richard hired me because at the May 12 event, he accidentally left his Visa card on a table, next to the phone, and someone copied down the card number. That person left the card there and then, later on, used the card number to make three $200 donations, in Richard's name, to the House or Senate campaigns of Romney, King, and Pelosi. I'm asking everyone if they can provide any observations from that May 12 event—no matter how minor—as even the smallest piece of information might possibly help me identify the culprit."

Roger thought for a few seconds, then he responded, "As I recall, I did see a small table somewhere near the back of the room. But I really didn't see anything unusual. I'll make the obvious observation that whoever used the card to make those contributions is clearly nonpartisan. He gave Richard's money to a Republican, an independent, and a Democrat. But Richard did get the money back from Visa, right?"

Amy nodded. "That is indeed correct. Did you notice the credit card next to the phone?"

He smiled. "Frankly, I didn't even notice that there was a phone on the table. I was too busy hobnobbing with the candidates. You know, most of them sounded very intelligent and caring."

She laughed. "Actually, I have found that most candidates can memorize enough material so that they can appear intelligent and caring when they are actually dumb and disinterested." Now everyone laughed, then Amy continued, "So no one there acted in any way suspicious or unusual?"

He shook his head. "No, it was a fun event, a friendly event. I wasn't thinking about looking for suspicious activity, so it makes sense that I didn't notice any. I wish I could be of more assistance to Richard."

"Roger, you're a Democrat—like me—right?"

"Yep, most of the people in our club are Democrats, but we welcome Republicans and members of the minor parties. However, I have actually voted for a few Republicans. For example, I voted for Bloomberg for mayor in 2005."

The interview ended, and after Roger had departed, Jeremy immediately spoke up. "Mike Bloomberg became a Republican only as a strategic move to get nominated for mayor. After he finished as mayor, he switched back and spoke as a Hillary supporter at the 2016 Democratic Convention. So I seriously doubt that Roger ever supported a real Republican.

"And just like with Martin, Roger doesn't realize that those three contributions were all of the type that a sophisticated Democrat would make, as opposed to a nonpartisan voter. Actually, it's even worse. He thinks Angus King is really a political independent, whereas even I knew King votes with the Democrats."

Amy nodded. "Well, to be fair to Roger, King is officially an independent. But I agree with you; I'm now officially withdrawing my statement that the club members are sophisticated. It's probably closer to the opposite of that."

At two thirty, Amy and Jeremy welcomed John Tamora to their table. He wore a white shirt and a dark gray sports jacket. John was in his late forties, short, and thin. And he looked angry. Amy began with her usual opening presentation.

"Richard hired me because at the May 12 event, he accidentally left his Visa card on a table, next to the phone, and someone copied down the card number. That person left the card there and then, later on, used the card number to make three $200 donations, in Richard's name, to the House or Senate campaigns of Romney, King, and Pelosi. I'm asking everyone if they can provide any observations from that May 12 event—no matter how minor—as even the smallest piece of information might possibly help me identify the culprit."

John shook his head. "Amy, I only came here this afternoon because I couldn't believe this was actually happening. Someone pulled off this silly scam, and Richard has gone off his rocker. The three candidates will end up not getting the money. Richard will get all of it back. I blame Richard for this whole thing. He's trying to divert attention from his stupidity in leaving his card on a table in a public place.

"And I'll bet Richard secretly believes that one of us from the club did it. That would fit perfectly with the rest of his character. From what Richard told me, he suspected his girlfriend of some kind of misbehavior, so he broke it off with her. In most ways, he's a nice guy, but this suspicion stuff is his big flaw."

Amy laughed. "Who knows, John, maybe you have a point, but I'm just trying to find the culprit who fraudulently used Richard's card number. And if you can recall anything from that event, maybe it could help me."

"Well, at the banquet hall, I actually remember seeing two phones, one near the back of the hall and one on the side, by the windows. Which phone was where Richard left his card?"

Amy had a surprised look on her face. "I don't know which phone Richard was using. This is the first time I've heard from anyone that there were two phones. Did you see anyone hanging around either of the phones or looking suspicious in any way?"

"There was one man with a full beard by the rear phone, and I recall he was still there the next time I was looking that way a few minutes later. But I can't provide any further description of the guy. I guess you could do some further checking with some other guests, and maybe you can find out who he was."

Amy nodded and smiled. "Thanks so much. I appreciate you giving me that information. Would you have selected all—or maybe one or two—of those three candidates if you were making campaign contributions?"

John shook his head. "No way! I only contribute to candidates—Democrats, of course—who are running for office where I would be one of their constituents. This year, I would only contribute—and I did, in fact, contribute—to Alexandria Ocasio-Cortez. She's running for the House seat for my district in the June Democratic primary, trying to unseat the long-term Democrat incumbent, Joe Crowley, who is currently the chair of the House Democratic Caucus. In 2002, Crowley voted in favor of authorizing President Bush's Iraq invasion, so I have not been a fan of Crowley since then."

"John," she replied sheepishly, "I've never heard of Alexandria what's her name." She turned to her husband. "Jerry, have you ever heard of her?" He shook his head.

John nodded. "That doesn't surprise me. But hopefully, Alexandria Ocasio-Cortez will win the primary, and then it won't take very long until everyone will sure as hell be aware of her!"

The interview ended, and Amy again looked to Jeremy for feedback.

"Sweetheart, my first observation is that I've got to check out this Alexandria lady. Secondly, it looks like John is the only one so far who realizes that Richard views him and the other three as prime suspects. Other than that, I've got nothing. Also, as usual, you always use the exact same initial presentation of why you were hired."

"That's true, I make sure to use the same opening. But, Jerry, what about the fact that there seem to have been two phones in the banquet hall? That could be really big!"

Her husband looked confused. "But, sweetheart, that seems to me to have no significance whatsoever."

She smiled. "I'd say you're sure as hell right about that. I was just joshing you." They both burst out laughing.

After they calmed down, Amy continued, "John is also the first one who's acting pretty annoyed that Richard hired me to investigate the fraudulent card charges. Of course, he could be faking anger to make himself appear to be innocent."

"Sweetheart, in that case, John is an excellent actor."

She nodded. "I can't argue with you on that; his anger was very believable."

Malcolm Gintell showed up at five past three for Amy's final interview. He was in his fifties, the oldest of the foursome, and he was wearing exercise clothes. "Sorry for my appearance, but I rushed here directly from the gym."

Amy, of course, didn't care how he was dressed. "No worries, let me get straight down to the nitty-gritty. Richard hired me because at the May 12 event, he accidentally left his Visa card on a table, next to the phone, and someone copied down the card number. That person left the card there and then, later on, used the card number to make three $200 donations, in Richard's name, to the House or Senate campaigns of Romney, King, and Pelosi. I'm asking everyone if they can provide any observations from that May 12 event—no matter how minor— as even the smallest piece of information might possibly help me identify the culprit."

"Well, Amy, maybe I can contribute one significant observa- tion. I had my eye on an attractive woman standing in the rear of the room, speaking to another lady near the table with the phone. For the entire time I was watching her—maybe between five and ten minutes—a man with a thick gray beard was stand- ing right next to that table. I did not see him using the phone. He was just standing there, possibly waiting for a good time to unobtrusively snatch Richard's credit card from the table and take down the card number, then return the card to the table."

"Malcolm, did you actually see the credit card on the table?"

"No, I never actually looked directly at the table; I was looking at the woman. I'm just surmising that the card had been on the table because Richard said he had left it there."

"Can you provide any additional description of the bearded man?"

"Well, he was relatively short and pretty chubby. And he looked to be in his forties or fifties. That's about all I can say."

Amy nodded. "Well, you've given me an excellent description. I really appreciate it. What do you think of the three candidates I mentioned who received the contributions using Richard's card?"

"Yeah, that combination makes no sense whatsoever to me. I can't imagine anyone making political contributions to all three."

The interview ended, and Amy smiled at her husband. "Jerry, it's over; what are your final thoughts?"

"Well, Malcolm again confirmed that these guys are not politically sophisticated. Of course, you had the advantage of being politically tutored by your progressive Democrat parents from a young age."

"Yeah, Jerry, that certainly is true. Any other observations?"

"You and Spy4U can make inquiries and possibly identify the bearded man. He was definitely acting suspiciously."

Amy shook her head. "But how would that bearded man know how to find Richard's address?"

"I don't know, but maybe there's some way he could do so."

She smiled. "I could debate that question with you, but I already know, with 98 percent certainty, which of the four friends fraudulently used Richard's Visa card."

Jeremy was dumbfounded. "What? You know this based on today's interviews? And from where did you get the specific figure 98 percent?"

"You know full well where I got the specific figure 98 percent. I made it up; it sounded good." They both laughed. "And, of course, I know who the culprit is based on today's interviews. You were here for all four interviews, so you should know too."

"Sweetheart, you're joshing me again, right?"

"Wrong. I'm absolutely serious. When Richard arrives at three thirty, I'll tell him the case is solved and lay it all out for him."

"Well, before Richard shows up, how about you laying it all out for me?"

She nodded. "Okay, here goes. If I tell a politically aware resident of Queens—in particular, any one of the four friends, whether or not he's sophisticated—that someone made contributions to Romney, King, and Pelosi, the friend would immediately know who Romney and Pelosi were. But who would he think I was referring to with regard to the name King?

"Certainly *not* Senator Angus King of Maine—even if the friend had actually heard of Angus King, which, having spoken to them today, I now seriously doubt, at least with regard to some of them. Of course, the one friend who made the contribution to Senator King obviously did indeed know all about him.

"The man named King whom the friends who are not the culprit would assume I was referring to would almost certainly be Representative Peter King, a moderate Republican—like Romney—who has represented parts of Nassau and Suffolk Counties on Long Island in the House for the past fifteen years.

"Nassau County is right next to Queens County. Peter King frequently appears on local and national TV news programs. He is one of the most visible and well-known Republicans in the New York City Metropolitan Area.

"And yet one of the friends knew that the King I was referring to is an independent—not a Republican and not a Democrat. This friend knew I was referring to Angus King. He knew that because he is the one who made the contribution to Angus King using Richard's credit card number.

"Jerry, do you remember which friend referred to King as an independent?"

He smiled. "Yes, I think I do; it was Roger, right?"

"Right. Roger referred to the three recipients as a Republican, an independent, and a Democrat. So I am 98—oh, what the heck, make it 99—percent confident that Roger is the culprit."

"But, sweetheart, the first recipient you mentioned was Romney. Couldn't Roger have therefore simply assumed that the King you mentioned right after Romney was also running for Senate?"

She shook her head. "No way! First of all, the third recipient was Pelosi, who everyone knows is in the House. And second, in my presentation, I said the contributions were to House or Senate campaigns. I actually said House first. But good try."

He nodded. "Yeah, you're right. So have you come to any conclusion regarding the answer to the big question, namely why did Roger do it? As we said, he obtained no benefit, and Richard lost nothing."

"I think Roger has some mental health problems; he probably did it because he got a charge out of doing it. Of course, I'm not a mental health professional—not that I trust those guys too much either—so I'm just guessing. If I'm right, then Roger has probably pulled off stunts like this before. If I'm wrong, your guess regarding Roger's motive is as good as mine."

He nodded. "Makes sense. And I guess it doesn't matter. I think Richard just wants to know who did it so he can avoid being too close with that person." At this point, Jeremy finished consuming his cinnamon coffee cake.

Richard arrived at three thirty and took a seat at their table. "So how did the interviews go?"

Amy smiled. "Well, there's some bad news and some good news. The bad news is that John—but probably not the others—figured out that you strongly suspect that one of the four club members is the culprit. The good news is that I am 99 percent confident that I have identified the culprit, and it is not John. It's Roger."

Richard appeared stunned. "You're kidding, right?"

Amy laughed. "No, I'm serious; the case is solved." She explained in detail how she identified Roger as the one who used Richard's card number.

"Amy, you are absolutely unbelievable!"

"Well, I set a trap, and Roger fell right into it. That didn't have to happen."

"True, but there's an explanation for why you're so lucky, aside from the fact that you're a brilliant detective."

Amy's face started turning red.

"A few minutes ago, I bumped into John on Northern Boulevard. It was after you had interviewed him. He did tell me that he was pretty annoyed that I didn't choose to simply forget the whole thing, but then he said he was very surprised to discover that he actually enjoyed speaking to you. He said you were nothing like what he imagined a detective to be.

"That—besides you being a great detective—is why you are so lucky so often. People enjoy talking to you, and because of that, they say things to you that they shouldn't say."

Now Amy's face was bright red. "Richard, thanks for the compliment. So what will you now do with this information regarding Roger?"

"For me, knowing who did it is the big thing. It provides a sort of peace of mind, which, for me, is much more important than the money. Of course, I'll also be more careful when I'm around Roger."

Richard again profusely thanked Amy and also thanked Jeremy; then he left the restaurant. Jeremy smiled. "Sweetheart, putting aside all those nice compliments from Richard, you were pretty damn lucky, weren't you. If Roger had failed to mention that one of the three candidates is an independent—which could easily have happened—then you would have had no backup plan to solve the case, would you?"

She smiled back. "Jerry, you're sure as hell right about that. I needed one of them to say something to indicate they knew that candidate King referred to Senator King from Maine. That would incriminate them. If it didn't happen, I think I probably would have had to give up."

"Don't you often get a cash bonus for solving cases like this?"

"Yeah, and I only find out about any such bonus when and if I solve the case. However, here, Richard is a prolific client of Spy4U; he's hired us for multiple cases. So Mr. Murray would not attempt to negotiate a bonus deal, but would just tell Richard it's entirely up to him. So we'll have to wait and see what he does."

"What's next on the agenda?"

"Mr. Murray is asking some of our Spy4U people to see if they can identify and locate Jasper."

"Is that the guy Mary saved from being hit by a car?"

"Yep, that's the one. We have to see if he actually made Mary his sole heir and whether some relative of Jasper's may have had a good motive to kill Mary on April 14."

Tuesday, May 29, 2018

At eleven in the morning, Chester knocked on Amy's office door. "Amy, I have the information you asked for regarding people named Jasper living in Noble Grove and surrounding towns. They could only find one Jasper." He handed her a sheet of paper. "It's all there."

Amy thanked her boss, checked out the report, and then phoned her husband. "Jerry, we have probably identified Jasper. His last name is Waggoner. He lives in Noble Grove and is seventy-three years old. He and a business partner, Charles Danzig, run an independent insurance agency. He has, to the best of our knowledge, married only once, had no children, and was divorced in 1987. His parents are dead, and he had only one sibling, a younger brother, Clark, who died in 2005 in an auto accident. Clark had two children; both are daughters. Their names are Joan and Karen; both have apparently never married and have no children. That's basically all we have."

"Sweetheart, how do you know you have the right Jasper?"

"We don't know for sure. Jasper Waggoner was the only Jasper our people could find who lived in or near Noble Grove. That certainly is not conclusive proof that he's the one. Obviously, I have to try to obtain an interview with Jasper, or with Charles

Danzig, his business partner. I'll work on it this afternoon, and I'll update you when I get home."

When Amy got home, she kissed her husband and gave him the news. "Jerry, I couldn't contact Jasper, but Charles Danzig has agreed to meet with me tomorrow at noon. I told his administrative assistant I needed Mr. Danzig's help to possibly stop a killer from striking again. She put me on hold for well over a minute and finally got back on and gave me the appointment."

Jeremy was confused. "Striking again? Did you make that up, or is it true?"

"Sure, it's true. Let's say that Karen, who is one of Jasper's nieces, killed Mary so that she would be a beneficiary in Jasper's will. Now before Karen can actually receive any money, Jasper must die. Therefore, Karen may want to hasten Jasper's death."

He nodded. "You know, you're right. Jasper may be in grave danger. But do we know if Jasper is still alive? Maybe he died some time ago. Those people searches are not up to date, as you previously pointed out."

Amy smiled. "That's possible. And I always appreciate it when you quote me to make a point. Anyhow, I expect to find out what's going on with Jasper when I speak to Charles tomorrow. His office is located in downtown Noble Grove, although that could be an oxymoron." They both laughed.

Wednesday, May 30, 2018

As Amy had suspected, there was really no downtown in Noble Grove, New Jersey. The only other business on the same street as Noble Insurance Partners was a shoe repair shop. Amy parked right in front of the small one-story Noble Insurance building and walked in.

There was no waiting room and no receptionist. Only two desks. One had the nameplate Jasper Waggoner, and there was no one seated there. The other had the nameplate Charles Danzig, so Amy assumed the man appearing to be in his sixties, with almost no hair left on his head, was indeed Charles.

Charles rose, shook Amy's hand, and motioned for her to take a seat. Then he returned to his seat at the desk. "Ms. Bell, you said you work for Spy4U Services."

"That's correct, but please call me Amy," she interrupted.

"Sure, and I'm Charles. You said someone may get killed if we don't act?"

"Well, that is a distinct possibility. Let me explain the situation. We believe that several years ago, your partner, Jasper Waggoner, was saved from being hit by a car by a woman named Mary Rackner. Can you confirm that?"

Charles had a surprised look on his face. "Why, yes! That happened in 2006. How do you know about that?"

"I know about that because one of Mary's best friends, a woman named Christine Longley, told me about it. Christine said that Jasper told Mary he would make a donation to a charity in her honor. He also said he was so grateful to Mary for probably saving his life that as he was not too fond of his relatives, he would make her the sole beneficiary of his will. Mary told Jasper not to do that.

"Charles, my question is, did Jasper put Mary into his will, and if so, was she the sole beneficiary?"

"Amy, I'm not the best person to answer your question. I can only tell you what Jasper told me. But I can't refer you to Jasper, because he has been in the hospital, in a coma—due to natural causes—for the past two months. The doctors tell me his coma is irreversible, and he may die at any time, or he may possibly go on this way for quite a while. Jasper left no instructions for something like this, and he has no relatives close enough to approve removing the feeding tubes. Of course, there have been a few miracles where people woke up from comas that were supposed to be irreversible.

"As far as I am aware, Jasper did, indeed make Mary the sole beneficiary of his will. When Jasper dies, Mary will inherit a few million dollars, which is what Jasper told me he was worth a couple of years ago."

Amy nodded. "Okay, Charles, here's why I contacted you. On April 14 of this year, Mary was murdered in her backyard in Ferman Township, New Jersey. She was shot four times with a handgun." Charles moaned and lowered his head into his hands as Amy continued, "I came to the realization that with Mary dead, one of Jasper's relatives—who has now become an heir—may have been Mary's killer and would now be motivated to kill Jasper so as to collect the money from Jasper's estate.

"Given that Jasper is in the hospital, in a coma, I guess the relative, even if they murdered Mary, will probably not attempt to kill Jasper at this point but will, instead, just wait for him to die. Regardless, all relatives who may inherit are clearly major suspects in Mary's murder. I understand that there are just two relatives, namely two nieces. Am I correct?"

"Yes, Amy, you are correct. They are Joan and Karen Waggoner. They are both in their early thirties; Joan is two years older. I think they both live in Manhattan. Of course, it is possible that Jasper put a provision in his will that if Mary cannot inherit, all his money goes to charity. His lawyer is Oscar Lewis, whose office is a few blocks from here. But frankly, I don't think Oscar will tell you anything regarding Jasper's will while Jasper is still alive, even though he's in a coma.

"It's also possible that contrary to what he said to me, Jasper did not make Mary his sole beneficiary, or maybe he did not even leave Mary anything in his will. And again, I'm pretty sure that Oscar won't tell you anything about what's in the will."

Amy nodded. "Of course, it's not what's in Jasper's will that matters; it's what the nieces believe is in the will—or even what they believe might be in the will. Did Jasper tell them he shut them out?"

"As far as I am aware, Jasper never discussed the contents of his will with his nieces. They were not on good terms and rarely spoke; sometimes there were several years between conversations."

"Charles, do you know why Jasper was on bad terms with his nieces?"

"Yes, it was because they were smoking marijuana and were very proud of it. This started when they were teenagers. They openly proclaimed its merits—not just for medical purposes but for recreation. And they have continued touting marijuana right up till now, unless they've very recently had a change of heart. Jasper could not accept this behavior. Personally, I would be very surprised if Jasper ever spoke to them about Mary or about his will. But, of course, they theoretically could have somehow found out. Jasper may have told a friend who then told a friend and so on. After all, he told me, but I never told anyone else, until today, while speaking to you.

"You should try to arrange to meet with them. Don't tell them they're suspects in a murder. And I won't tell anyone about our conversation. By the way, in case you're interested, if Jasper dies, his half of our company automatically comes to me, so I would own 100 percent of Noble Insurance Partners."

Amy smiled. "Thanks for telling me. I certainly will contact the two nieces. Do they have any past history of violence, as far as you know?"

"No, not at all. They were probably too high on marijuana to attack anyone." They both laughed, and, shortly thereafter, Amy departed. She had lunch at Wendy's and then headed for Spy4U. She did a brief computer search and then phoned her husband.

"Jerry, Jerry! It's just like I said. Charles, Jasper's business partner, said Jasper told him he made Mary his sole beneficiary. Jasper was not on speaking terms with his only relatives, his two nieces, because they were heavy marijuana users and proud of it.

"And guess what? Jasper has been in an irreversible coma since this past March! So clearly, one of those nieces may have murdered Mary. Charles did say he doubts that Jasper told them about Mary saving him or about what he was doing with his will. But he admitted they might have found out from a friend of a friend of Jasper's—you know what he meant, right?"

"Yeah, I know what he meant; that's how gossip works. Jasper confided in a friend, who then told someone else, and so on, until it finally got back to one of the nieces."

"Smart boy! In any case, I think I've located both Joan and Karen Waggoner in Manhattan. Charles had said he thinks both nieces live in Manhattan, so it is indeed probably them. I'll see if I can phone or possibly email them and, hopefully, set up a meeting. They don't have any idea that I suspect that one of them is a murderer. I'll tell them the meeting is regarding Jasper. When I get home, I'll update you on the situation. Bring home a large pepperoni and mushroom pizza for dinner."

After dinner, Amy provided the update. "I have an interview with Joan at her apartment tomorrow morning at eleven. It's at a swanky address on Park Avenue. After that, I'll meet with Karen for lunch at Lambert's Diner, right here in Greenwich Village, at one fifteen. She said she's bringing along a very good friend. From the way Karen said it, I presume it's her significant other."

Jeremy smiled. "Sweetheart, the way you described it, I'll bet that Karen's significant other is a woman."

She nodded. "Yeah, now that you mention it, I think you may be right. I guess I'll find out tomorrow."

"Are these two women currently your prime suspects?"

"Jerry, I don't know how to answer that. They had no motive to kill Mary unless they knew the whole story about her saving Jasper and then Mary being named as the the sole beneficiary in Jasper's will. Everyone agrees that's possible—based on the gossip theory—but is it likely?

"And in that case, the warning letters, arriving shortly before the murder, are just a coincidence. We have discussed that possibility, but again, is it likely?

"So we would need two unlikely events to have both occurred. Jerry, you are the probability genius. What's the chances of both of those two occurring?"

"Using probability terminology, if the two events are independent of each other, as seems to be the case here, we would multiply the individual probabilities. So for example, if the probability of each event, taken separately, is 10 percent, then the probability that both events occurred is 10 percent times 10 percent, which equals a 1 percent probability."

"Well, regardless of the low probability, I'll be meeting with them tomorrow. I'm interested to hear what they have to say. I'll probably come back here directly after the second interview and work from home. After all, Lambert's Diner is only a few blocks away."

Thursday, May 31, 2018

At 10:55 a.m., the uniformed doorman took Amy's information and phoned Joan Waggoner to confirm her permission for Amy to enter the building. Having received a positive reply, he escorted Amy to the elevator, which took her to the twenty-eighth floor. The nameplate on Joan's apartment door said Marquez-Waggoner. Amy rang the bell and was welcomed in by a very attractive woman, five foot six, dressed casually. They shook hands and agreed to use first names.

The apartment was large and lavishly furnished. There were several paintings on the wall that Amy thought could be originals. "Joan, could that possibly be an original Dali?" Amy inquired, as they took seats in the living room.

"Why, yes, you're very sophisticated! May I get you a snack or something to drink?"

"No, thanks, I'm actually having lunch at Lambert's Diner with Karen at one fifteen."

"Right, she did mention that to me. So what brings you here regarding my uncle Jasper?"

"Well, as you know, Jasper is the co-owner of an independent insurance agency. And as I'm sure you also know, Jasper is currently in a coma and may die in the near future."

Joan looked very surprised. "Oh, gosh, I was not aware of that. I'll explain after you finish what you were saying."

"Sure. An organization of independent insurance agents—I can't mention their name—is thinking of having an event officially honoring Jasper. This would occur after he passes away. They retained my firm to speak to his friends, acquaintances, and relatives to confirm that it would be appropriate to bestow this honor and to also get some details regarding his life."

Joan nodded. "Well, I guess Karen and I will not be the people to talk to about how deserving Jasper is of being honored. He had old-fashioned views about how people should conduct themselves in their private lives, and he carried them to the extreme. In our case, we have enjoyed smoking marijuana ever since our midteens. We are not apologetic about this. Our parents were not pleased, but they were somewhat understanding and nonjudgmental.

"Jasper was the opposite of understanding. He openly condemned us and was unwilling to even discuss this matter with us in a civilized way. He ended up hardly ever speaking to us— or having any contact at all—for the past fifteen years. When one of us would leave Jasper a voice mail message or send an email, he would usually not respond. That's why I did not know about Jasper being near death, in a coma. I presume that Karen is also unaware; of course, you can ask her this afternoon."

Amy smiled. "Well, Joan, it's obvious that smoking marijuana has not affected your financial situation." They both laughed. "Would you say there have been any negative effects?"

"Other than Jasper shunning us, no negative effects. I am aware that marijuana has had very bad effects on others, but not us. Maybe we're just lucky. Anyhow, to be fair, marijuana did not help me get to this financial situation. Actually, I married a very wealthy man."

Now Amy was surprised. "Oh, I had heard that you and Karen both were not married; I see that I've received erroneous information."

"I would say half of your information was erroneous. Karen is not married—at least technically speaking." She flashed a big smile. "But I've been married for the past eight years to Alex Marquez. He's twenty years older than me, and we first met at a party where we were both smoking marijuana."

Amy broke into hysterical laughter. "Joan, I'm sorry. But you are the biggest marijuana success story in American history! I am nominating you for the Timothy Leary Lifetime Achievement Award!" Now Joan burst into laughter.

When everyone had calmed down, Amy continued, with a question. "Does Alex still smoke marijuana?"

"Yes, but to a lesser degree; he never smoked marijuana as much as I did. Oh my god, you're so much fun to talk to. I'm saying things I shouldn't. Don't tell anyone what I told you about Alex. Don't even tell anyone we're married. I have kept that private. Of course, Karen knows, but none of my relatives and very few of my acquaintances know. At his job—he manages a billion-dollar investment fund—and in most other public activities, I'm known as Joan Marquez."

"Joan, do you have your own career?"

"Yes, I took some business and finance classes at college, and after we were married, Alex schooled me a bit more in that area. So now I'm a financial writer; I submit articles to newspapers and magazines. I work from home.

"But, Amy, please don't interpret anything I say to indicate that Jasper shouldn't be honored for his lifelong success in the insurance business. I know he always did very well in that area."

After a few final pleasantries, Amy departed and took the subway home. She opened her apartment door at twelve fifteen and surprised her husband. "Sweetheart, I thought you also had a lunch meeting."

"Yeah, but that's at one fifteen, and the diner is only a ten-minute walk from here. Anyhow, the probability that Joan killed Mary is about one millionth of 1 percent." Amy related all the details. "Joan sure as hell does not need Jasper's money."

"What about Karen? Is she rich too?"

"I doubt it. Joan indicated, with one of her comments, that Karen is not married but does have a long-term significant other. We'll see real soon if you're right about this person being a woman."

When Amy arrived at Lambert's Diner wearing her red scarf, two women were seated on a sofa in the entrance lobby. They both rose, and the thin five-foot-seven brunette extended her hand. "Hi, Amy, I'm Karen—Joan said to use first names." They shook hands as the other woman, a chubby five-foot-four blonde, rose. "And this is my very good friend—aw, to hell with all that, my significant other for the past five years, and we intend to get married soon—Paula Frankman."

"Hi, Paula, pleasure to meet you." They shook hands, and then the hostess escorted the trio to a table, where they ordered food and drinks. Amy started the conversation. "So how did you two guys get together?"

Karen responded, "We were both teaching as music lecturers in the Music and Art Department at Borough of Manhattan Community College. In fact, we're both still teaching there, and this semester we both arranged to teach four days a week and be off on Thursdays. We noticed each other, if you know what I mean, at a faculty meeting in March 2013. I moved in with Paula that June.

"Joan called me and told me you were doing research on my uncle Jasper for an insurance-related organization that is considering honoring him. Joan also told me you said Jasper is now in an irreversible coma and will likely die soon. How can I possibly help you?"

"Well, Joan said that due to your marijuana use, Jasper basically shunned you two for the past fifteen years. Can you elaborate on that?"

Karen smiled. "One thing I can add was that on the rare occasions—maybe once every three or four years—when Joan or I emailed Jasper or left a phone mail message and he really had to reply, he would be very brief, and he always threw in some comment, like we can still stop now before it destroys us. He also occasionally sent us information on how to join Marijuana Anonymous."

"Marijuana Anonymous?" interrupted Amy. "You're joking, right?"

"No," Paula responded, "that really is the name of the organization. They're similar to Alcoholics Anonymous. They have meetings and also a twelve-step program. Of course, it's for people for whom marijuana use is a harmful problem in their lives. On the other hand, marijuana is a positive for our lives."

Amy nodded. "I understand what you're saying. So, Karen, would it be fair to say that Jasper truly cared about your welfare, although his caring may have been misguided?"

She shook her head. "I would have agreed with that, except for the fact that Jasper wanted nothing to do with us. It was all on his side. We would have been happy to travel to Noble Grove to visit with him. We could have enjoyed each other's company. We could have learned from him, and he could have learned from us. That's the way it was supposed to be. And now, as I just found out today, Jasper has lapsed into in an irreversible coma, and it's too late."

Amy nodded. "You make an excellent point. On another topic, do both of you have tenure in the Music and Art Department at BMCC?"

"Yes," answered Karen, "we do, with the opportunity for future promotion to the professor level."

During lunch, Karen and Paula told Amy about their music backgrounds and their classes at BMCC. After finishing their desserts, they said goodbye, and Amy walked home and gave her husband an update.

"So, Jeremy, you were right on target regarding Karen's significant other being a woman. Karen and Paula seem to be very happy together. They plan to marry soon. They have successful careers in higher education. Karen had hardly any contact with Jasper over the past fifteen years. I regret to say I'm pretty sure I've come up empty here. Karen is almost surely not Mary's killer. Do you concur?"

He nodded. "Yes, I do. Of course, you should verify that Karen and Paula are, indeed, tenured lecturers in the Department of Music and Art at BMCC."

"Of course, I'll do that. I always attempt to verify what people—particularly suspects—tell me in interviews. But I very much doubt that they lied."

"So, sweetheart, what's next?"

"I think I'll try to meet with Aaron Ryman, who Mary listed as her lawyer. I agree with Matthew, the trustee I interviewed last, that if Mary was bullying and insulting to people in Ferman Township, Aaron may be the one who is most likely to be aware of this behavior."

"Do you think Mary really was a bully, or was that other trustee, Neil—the one who told you about Mary's bullying—simply making a mountain out of a molehill?"

Amy was contemplative. "Well, Christine says no bullying. Anna, the principal, says no bullying. Matthew says no bullying. Polly and Peggy, the other trustees, said nothing about bullying. And Peggy told me she's leaving the board at the end of June. There was no reason for her to make excuses for Mary.

"Of course, if there was no bullying, I won't be able to find any new suspects. I'll be left with a female parent—which female parent, out of hundreds, I have no idea—as the likely killer. And I'm pretty sure that almost none of those parents would be willing to talk to me. So as with the police, I'm apt to be left with a female shoeprint, with no way to identify the owner of the shoe."

"Sweetheart, I have a feeling—which you have expressed in several previous murder cases—that we're missing something very important."

Amy nodded vigorously. "Jerry, I think you're sure as hell right about that!"

Saturday, June 2, 2018

While Jeremy was enjoying his weekly tennis match, Amy was joining Denise Bromfield for lunch at Delmore's, a fancy restaurant on the Upper West Side. Denise had adamantly demanded to pay for the both of them, as Amy had recently cleared up a touchy situation faced by Denise's husband, Gary.

Brought up by a poor single mother, Denise never attended college. However, she was a prolific reader, on a multitude of topics, but especially books on business and finance. She also grew up to be a very beautiful woman. Denise spent a number of years as a waitress, finally getting a good job serving meals and beverages to employees of a large company in their executive "cafeteria"—clearly a misnomer—at the firm's Manhattan headquarters.

One day, she served lunch to the company's CEO. Later that afternoon, the CEO—who was twice her age—returned to the cafeteria to ask Denise out to dinner. Within a few weeks, they were married. When the CEO died, Denise inherited a sum of money in the low nine figures. She founded a charity, Return to Learn, and became its president.

Amy first met Denise when she interviewed Denise as part of a Spy4U murder investigation. In order to solve the murder, Amy had to uncover some of Denise's deepest, darkest, personal secrets. However, all was forgiven, and Amy and Denise became very close friends.

They greatly respected each other's intellectual talents. Amy felt that Denise was the smartest woman she had ever met. Denise felt that Amy was the best sleuth in the world and someone with whom she could always be her real self. Indeed, Amy considered Denise to be her second-best girlfriend, after Cathy.

Amy was instrumental in getting Denise together with her second husband, Gary Bromfield, a professor of Russian history at North Jersey College. Amy and Jeremy had taken vacations with the Bromfields and had frequently visited them at their lavish Upper West Side condo.

"So, Denise, what esoteric topic are you and Gary discussing—or debating—lately?"

Denise smiled. "Amy, do you really want to know?"

"Yes, I do."

"We've been discussing whether Kliment Voroshilov was actually as dumb as Stalin and the other members of the Politburo thought he was. Of course, he was so dumb that he survived Stalin's multiple purges and became president of the Soviet Union during the 1950s. Oh, and he also had the military rank of Marshal of the Soviet Union, which was the highest rank."

Amy laughed. "We should all be so dumb."

"Okay, Amy, enough of that. Tell me about an interesting case you're working on."

Amy gave Denise an overview of her current murder case, referring to Mary as Barbara, as she had done with Cathy. "So, Denise, what do you think?"

"Okay, I'll stick my neck out. In my opinion, the idea that there is no connection between the warning letters and the murder is preposterous. Some claimed coincidences are simply not plausible. Now I am in no position to tell you what, specifically, is the connection. That job is up to you.

"The other thing that stands out is the question of whether or not Barbara bullied and insulted people. That is a very important question because if she did, then it creates a whole new bunch of suspects. So I suggest you pursue that question with as many people who dealt with her as possible."

Amy nodded. "What about the man she saved from being hit by a car and the issue of his will?"

"I agree with your analysis. Those nieces are doing too well in life to kill someone for an inheritance they may well not even get if he directed his money to go to charity if Barbara couldn't collect it. And furthermore, they probably didn't even know about Barbara.

"I also agree with you that the first niece is a shoo-in for the Timothy Leary Prize." They both laughed. "The two nieces are very lucky to be exceptions to the rule that marijuana use—particularly long-term and/or heavy use—can cause serious health issues.

"But let me reiterate, I am convinced that the warning letters are definitely not a coincidence and are probably the key to your investigation. Can I prove this? Of course not. But the idea that the letters are just a coincidence is—at least to me—simply absurd."

Amy smiled. "Okay, Denise why don't you now tell me what you really think?" They both broke into laughter.

When Amy got home, her husband had already returned from tennis. She reported to him Denise's insistence that the warning letters could not have been a mere coincidence. "So, Jerry, what do you think?"

He smiled. "Sweetheart, this is one of those situations where both sides are right. Denise is right that to have threatening letters like that, followed shortly thereafter by the murder of the threatened person, does not look like it could be a coincidence.

"But the other side of the argument is also right. As we've discussed, although Mary did not take the letters to the police, someone willing to kill her would have to assume that she would do so, and that would likely result in added police protection for Mary. Also, it is very unlikely that Mary would reverse herself on such an important issue due to threats, so the killer had lots to lose and nothing to gain by sending letters.

"It looks like what actually happened was that the killer lucked out regarding Mary not going to the police and then won by killing Mary, thereby likely putting the kibosh on her draconian proposal."

"So, Jerry, that's how you plan to leave it; everybody is right?"

He nodded. "Yes, except to again repeat my observation, which I have also heard you make several times regarding previous cases. We are missing something here. Something very important. Something critical to solving the case."

Amy laughed. "Jerry, I'll repeat my original response; you're sure as hell right about that. By the way, yesterday, I spoke to Oscar Lewis on the phone. Oscar is Jasper's lawyer, and he confirmed to me that he drafted Jasper's will and has it in his possession. However, that's all he was willing to tell me. Oscar said the contents of the will must remain totally confidential until Jasper dies."

"Sweetheart, I take it that doesn't surprise you."

"Correct, no surprise at all."

"So what's next?"

"I guess it's time to investigate whether Mary was a bully and insulted people in areas separate from the board of directors. As we've discussed, that could possibly be a motive for murder, totally apart from the academy. Christine gave me the name of the Teaneck community where Mary lived. If possible, I would like to speak to her neighbors there from ten years ago."

Monday, June 4, 2018

Southwest Teaneck Villas was a gated community located—surprise!—in the southwest section of Teaneck, New Jersey. Amy arrived at the gate at 1:45 p.m. and gave the guard the name of Morton Laubach, president of the community's board of directors as her sponsor for admission. She had spoken to Morton on the phone in the morning, and he had provided Amy's name to the guardhouse.

Morton had told Amy that one of his important jobs was to protect the privacy of the residents. If she wanted any kind of assistance from him in her investigation, she'd have to discuss it with him in person, and she should bring appropriate identification and documentation.

Amy was well aware that there are Internet websites which do address searches and people searches. But she felt that if she located Mary's neighbors in that way, they would refuse to talk to her, whereas with an "imprimatur" from Morton, she could get more cooperation from them.

When the gate was opened for her, Amy drove to the community center and found the board office. She had a two o'clock appointment with Morton, and he was waiting for her. Morton escorted Amy to a private meeting room, and they took seats.

They agreed to use first names, and Amy presented the situation, intentionally neglecting to mention the threatening letters just prior to Mary's murder.

"So, Morton, as it stands now, we have one of Mary's colleagues on the board who insists Mary was highly bullying and insulting, while others minimize the whole thing and say Mary was merely enthusiastic. Still others say that Mary did not bully or insult at all.

"Mary's good friend, Christine Longley, says Mary told her she had problems of some sort with her neighbors in Teaneck, but Mary did not elaborate further. I am hoping to be able to speak to some of Mary's neighbors from back then and find out whether she was, indeed, bullying and/or insulting towards them. If so, maybe they could provide some details to help me in my current investigation. If Mary did not exhibit bullying or insulting behavior, that would also be very helpful for me to know, as I would then concentrate my investigation in a different direction, with regard to the killer's motive."

Morton nodded. "I arrived here at Southwest Teaneck Villas only seven years ago. I had never heard of Mary Rackner—let alone that she had resided in our community—until you phoned me this morning. I will review our records and try to get in touch with Mary's neighbors from ten years ago. This may take a few days. I will inform them of the situation you have described and advise them to contact you if they are willing to meet with you or talk with you on the phone or communicate by email. That's the best I can do."

Amy thanked Morton for his assistance and drove home, stopping to get gas and also to make some purchases at Family

Dollar. She was slowed down by some very heavy traffic and didn't get home until four twenty-five.

Upon arrival, she kissed her husband and described her meeting in Teaneck. "Jerry, the whole thing was very frustrating. Maybe some neighbors will contact me, but I doubt it. Privacy of residents seems to be Morton's main concern, not solving a murder. Actually, I don't blame Morton. But if I get no responses, I'll have to try to locate the neighbors myself, which would probably make them even less apt to talk to me. But I'll have to try."

"Sweetheart, you can't believe that any of those neighbors from ten years ago are suspects in the murder, can you? If any of them was gonna kill Mary, they would have done it many years ago."

She shook her head. "No, of course not. I just want to get an idea of how bad her bullying and/or insulting was—assuming there was any. Of course, if the neighbors were, indeed, bullied by Mary, they may feel that if they speak to me about it, then they will become suspects. In any case, there are two things I can do to address my frustration. First, we can go out for steak dinner this evening at Ruth's Chris. Is that okay with you?"

Jeremy nodded and smiled. "Sure, Ruth's Chris is fine. And I can guess what thing number 2 is."

His wife licked her lips. "So I won't have to go over thing number 2; we'll just do it, for as long as it takes to relieve myself of all of my frustration."

At this point, the conversation was interrupted by the ringing of Amy's phone. "Ms. Bell, my name is Doreen Levitz. My husband, Craig, and I were next-door neighbors of Mary Rackner at Southwest Teaneck Villas for three years, right up to when she moved away in 2008. Morton Laubach says you are investigating Mary's murder."

Amy put on the speaker. "Thanks so much for phoning me. Please call me Amy, and I hope I can call you Doreen."

"Sure, Amy, I had no idea that Mary was murdered. Morton says that as part of your investigation, you want to know if Mary was a bully or insulted people. Is that correct?"

"Yes, that's right."

"To properly respond, I have to explain the role of our community's compliance officer."

Amy laughed. "Doreen, you sure do have to explain about the compliance officer. I've never heard of that position."

"Well, our community has a lot of common property, owned by all of us and not by any specific homeowner. We also have a community center, which hosts various community activities. We—actually our board of directors—hire a management company to run all the common areas.

"The management company—with the agreement of the board—makes up the rules and regulations for homeowner behavior in the common areas. The board also has regulations regarding what homeowners cannot do on their own property. For example, no political signs allowed. The management company—again with the agreement of the board—appoints a compliance officer, who goes around the community looking for violations of the rules. Violators can be fined, sometimes heavily, depending on the nature of the offense. Sometimes, for first-time, minor offenders, there is no fine, just a warning."

Amy laughed. "Doreen, that sounds very distasteful; sorry I'm laughing."

"Well, it gets worse. Residents can tattle on other residents to the compliance officer and ask the officer to investigate the alleged offense."

"Oh my god, Doreen, I would not want to live in a place like that."

"Actually, believe it or not, it's a very nice community in which to live. Some rules are necessary to preserve the beauty of the community and ensure successful operation of all the activities. I'm still living here; Craig passed away two years ago."

"Oh, Doreen, I'm so sorry."

"Thank you. In any case, Mary made a career of berating her neighbors for small rule violations and saying she'd report them to the compliance officer. And then she did, indeed, tattle on them to the compliance officer. Sometimes, she tattled to the compliance officer without first informing the offending neighbor that she planned to do so. She tattled on me for various minor offenses, most of which I had never even heard of. She must have carefully studied and memorized the rulebook.

"For example, I once poured out the remaining liquid contents of a container of Diet Pepsi—from which I had been drinking—onto the road. That's the gutter, not the sidewalk. I was too lazy to go back into my house and empty it into the sink. Mary saw this and screamed at me that she had made a video of my horrible infraction on her iPhone, and I should expect a fine from the compliance officer. She also called me a boor.

"Given the very brief amount of time it took me to empty the Diet Pepsi from the container onto the road, Mary must have started taking her video of me prior to the event, hoping that I would commit some sort of infraction.

"And yes, the compliance officer did inform me that a documented complaint had been made regarding the Diet Pepsi incident. Luckily, I received only a warning and was told that if anything like that happened again, I would be fined.

"I can think of only one plausible explanation for Mary's actions—not just with me but with several other residents that I was aware of at the time and doubtless with some others that I did not know about. Mary was a truly sick person who got her kicks by tattling and making her neighbors unhappy.

"Of course, we were all thrilled when Mary and her husband—a nice guy who seemed embarrassed by his wife's behavior—sold their house and moved away. I didn't want to know where she went or anything else about her from that point on. I won't say I'm happy to learn that Mary was murdered, as that would be unchristian. So I think I'll just leave it at that.

"I was very happy when Morton told me you were interested in hearing about Mary's behavior, as it gives me this opportunity to rant and let out all my pent-up grievances against her. I hope I don't sound like a nut."

Amy laughed. "No, not at all. You have provided the confirmation I've been looking for regarding Mary, and I'm very grateful for your rant—as you describe it." Now Doreen laughed, and the conversation ended shortly thereafter. Amy smiled at her husband.

"Well, Jerry, it looks like Neil Starkman, the board member who said Mary was a bully, was right—in spades! Let's see if any other Teaneck neighbors contact me about Mary."

"Sweetheart, please promise me you'll turn off your phone at Ruth's Chris and also during that other later activity."

She stroked him on the cheek. "That's an excellent suggestion; will do. You're such a smart boy!"

When they returned home from dinner, Amy checked her voice mail messages, and indeed there was a request for her to call Wendy Serrano, at a number with a Pennsylvania area code, regarding Mary. She punched in the number and turned on the speaker.

"Hello, this is Amy Bell, returning Wendy Serrano's call regarding Mary Rackner."

"Oh hi, I'm Wendy, and I hope we can use first names."

"Sure."

"Morton Laubach at Southwest Teaneck Villas emailed me and said you were investigating Mary's murder, which occurred this past April. He said you were interested in whether Mary bullied her neighbors in Teaneck before she moved away ten years ago.

"Well, she certainly did, and not just her neighbors. She would drive around the whole development—there are over a thousand homes—and photograph any infractions of the rules that she could find. And then she would send the photo to the compliance director so that the offending homeowner would be fined.

"I was one of her victims, and I recall other people in the community telling me Mary reported on them. In my case, I was running for local office, and for the week before election day, I put a poster up in the window of a room facing the street. It had my photo and the words, 'Vote Wendy Serrano for Councilwoman.'

"A week after election day—which was six days after I had removed the poster—I received a notice from the compliance officer. I was being fined $100 for putting up a political sign, in violation of rule number whatever. The notice included a photo of my poster, taken by Mary, who had reported my infraction to the officer. Note that I was not Mary's neighbor. I had been her neighbor, but a few years prior to this poster incident, I had moved to a different street in the community some distance away. I had a passing acquaintance with Mary from the period when we were neighbors.

"I understand the need for a community compliance officer, but what Mary did to me—and to others—was way out of bounds. When I bumped into her at a community function, I told her that, and she responded by saying that I was a shameful disgrace to the community, and the fine should been much higher than $100. I guess that's how Mary got her kicks in life—reporting on people and getting them fined.

"I moved to Pennsylvania several months before Mary left the community, as I understand it. I never heard anything about Mary after that until Morton told me you were investigating her murder."

Amy thanked Wendy for her help and then got off the phone. "Jerry, I may or not be contacted by other residents, but I have to say I'm very pleased and surprised, given Morton's emphasis on privacy and his telling me it could take several days to contact the neighbors. I'll have to send Morton an email thanking him profusely for his timely assistance."

Jeremy nodded. "You bet! I think Morton probably has a computer search algorithm for finding all the residents for a certain range of addresses during a certain period of time, say, 2000 to 2008. Then he probably has an easy way of sending all of them a group email. He just didn't want you to think he would do this for anyone who asked, because he wouldn't. He would have to be convinced this search was truly justified. Morton handled everything with you in exactly the right way."

"Jerry, you're absolutely right."

"Okay, sweetheart, what's next on the agenda?"

"I have to speak to Aaron Ryman. According to Matthew Birch—the board member Mary had a crush on—Aaron was Mary's attorney. He would be the logical person to tell me if Mary was filing complaints about any individuals or businesses in Ferman Township."

"Sweetheart, maybe Mary outgrew or swore off filing complaints when she moved to Ferman Township."

Amy smiled. "So you feel the leopard might have changed its spots. Seems very unlikely. Of course, in Ferman, Mary no longer lived in an organized community like Southwest Teaneck Villas, and she was pretty well separated from her neighbors. But still, I'm hoping that Mary may have continued her evil ways, of course with a different *modus operandi*, and that Aaron can provide the names of her victims in her new hometown."

"Then you think one of her Ferman bullying victims is the likely killer?"

She nodded. "If there are recent victims, then one of them may well have been enraged enough to kill her."

"So now you're back to saying the warning letters Mary received would be just a coincidence?"

She began stroking his cheek. "No, silly boy, those letters would not be just a coincidence. It would simply mean that the objectionable conduct the letters warned about was not Mary's academy proposal, but instead, Mary's bullying of the letter sender or of the sender's company."

He smiled. "Sweetheart, you're right, I hadn't thought of that. Of course, we're back to the observation that someone who'd be willing to kill Mary would surely assume that Mary would take the letters to the police, who would likely not only provide extra protection but would also try to identify the sender."

She continued stroking. "Yeah, I guess I'll have to go with the assumption that killers can be dumb." They both laughed.

"And now, it's time for me to again turn off my phone." Amy's hand moved down from her husband's cheek and into his pants. "I think I'll leave the phone off for about an hour and a half." Her hand had now located what it was searching for. "I no longer need to relieve any frustration regarding Morton, but I'm gonna require that amount of time to fully satisfy some of my other needs, slowly and methodically."

At this point, Jeremy was starting to feel some needs of his own, and he took appropriate action.

Wednesday, June 6, 2018

Aaron Ryman's law office in Ferman Township was in a small stand-alone white frame bungalow between a hardware store and a bar. At 11:20 a.m., Amy parked her car on the street a block away and walked over. She rang the doorbell, and a tall handsome man, appearing to be in his early forties opened the door and ushered her in. "Hi, Amy, I'm Aaron." They shook hands. Amy smiled and nodded to signify her approval of his use of first names. Aaron escorted her past the reception room and into his private office, where they took seats.

"Amy, I was intrigued by your email requesting a meeting. I'm delighted that you and your firm are investigating the murder of Mary Rackner. Everyone here in Ferman Township was shocked and enraged, particularly as it appears to have been connected to Mary's proposal to bolster academic excellence at the Ferman Academy. Please tell me how I can assist you with your investigation."

"Okay, Aaron, let me give you some background." Amy recounted what Neil Starkman had told her regarding Mary being a bully to other board members as well as insulting them. Then she repeated the stories told to her by two of Mary's former neighbors in Teaneck.

He was nonplussed. "I've had several conversations with other board members—although not with Neil—who were aware that I was Mary's attorney. They never said anything like that about Mary. Whenever I met with Mary, she was always friendly and enthusiastic—sometimes overly enthusiastic, but never bullying or insulting.

"With regard to Teaneck, you know that the residents are actually expected to abide by the rules. Of all the former neighbors Morton contacted—by the way, how many were there?"

She shook her head. "Sorry, Aaron. I have no idea how many, and I don't think Morton would want to tell me how many."

"Well, Amy, out of all those neighbors, only two have contacted you, right?"

"As of now, it's only two."

"And it was over ten years ago, right?"

"Right."

"So there's a decent chance that those two individuals knew they did wrong and have transformed this guilt into anger directed at Mary. Also, as so often happens over time, they are probably exaggerating Mary's behavior toward them to make it much nastier than it actually was."

"Aaron, are you saying that to the best of your knowledge, Mary was not making complaints against any residents or businesses here in the Ferman Township area?"

He paused for a few seconds before responding. "Well, not exactly."

Amy smiled. "Could you please elaborate?"

"Sure. There's a high-end ladies' clothing store owned by two local women a few blocks from here; its name is Ladies Choice. They have a seven-day, return-for-a-refund policy, provided the item of clothing is returned in the same condition as when it was bought. Mary and the store were having a dispute regarding some items she attempted to return for which they refused to refund the purchase price.

"There were actually a decent number of pieces of clothing involved—maybe five or six. Apparently, Mary purchased them all during the same store visit, and the store says that when she brought them back, they all had bad stains, and one of them had small tears in the fabric.

"Mary claimed that she was in a big rush when she bought the items, so she did not carefully check them before purchasing them. Then when she finally looked at them a few days later, she discovered that they all had those flaws, which is why she then attempted to return them.

"When it was clear that Ladies Choice was not going to budge on this issue, Mary picketed the store several times and handed out flyers to passersby. This occurred in late March and continued through early April of this year. The store was considering legal action against Mary—I'm not at all sure who would have won in court—but then Mary was murdered on April 14.

"Mary spoke to me only once about this situation. She swore on a stack of Bibles that she never did anything that could have caused any of the damage. And she noted that she never removed the price tags. I told her if it ever went to court, of course I would represent her, but of course it didn't come to that.

"I guess this either makes Mary a nasty bully or a seriously wronged victim. So if you want, you can say this confirms your bully theory. Personally, I would not agree with that. Regardless, I am not aware of any other incidents where Mary could be accused of bullying while living here."

Amy laughed. "So you're saying it's just a coincidence that Mary was picketing outside Ladies Choice after being denied a refund on stained and damaged clothes, then she received two warning letters, and then shortly thereafter, she was murdered?"

"Firstly, I have no idea whether the first warning letter to Mary arrived before or after she attempted to return the clothing she had purchased at Ladies Choice."

"That's a good point," interrupted Amy, then Aaron continued, "And, secondly, I would say it's vastly more likely that the letters and murder are connected to Mary's proposal regarding the academy, which was a very serious matter, affecting many people's lives. The Ladies Choice dispute was very minor, by comparison."

She nodded. "Aaron, that's also a good point. I would like to speak to someone at Ladies Choice. Do you know anyone there that you can contact, on my behalf, to arrange for me to meet with them regarding Mary's behavior?"

"Sure, Amy, I can try. My wife has purchased clothing at Ladies Choice, and I have accompanied her on some occasions to give my opinions—of course, only when asked. While there, I made the acquaintance of Laura DeRoy, one of the co-owners. I'll contact Laura and see if I can convince her to tell you her side of the story regarding the Mary dispute."

Amy thanked Aaron for everything, and shortly afterward, she departed for Spy4U, stopping along the way at KFC for lunch. When she arrived, she checked her messages and then phoned Christine.

"Hi, Christine, this is Amy Bell. I just spoke to Aaron Ryman, Mary's attorney, and he said there was a big dispute involving Mary and the clothing store Ladies Choice, regarding Mary's attempt to return for a refund some clothes that she had bought there. Do you know anything about that dispute?"

"Sorry, Amy, I never heard about any dispute between Mary and a clothing store—or any store, for that matter. As I had mentioned, Mary and I generally spoke about positive things. We got together for fun-type activities. That's the type of relationship we had."

Now Amy phoned her husband and recounted what Aaron had told her. "So, Jerry, what do you think?"

"I think you have to speak to Laura at Ladies Choice. Aaron acts as if the Mary dispute there was not serious enough to result in a murder, but he's wrong. Laura and the other co-owner likely had most of their life savings invested in the store, and they may have also taken out a business loan in order to get started. Their lives may well have been very seriously affected, and their entire economic status could have been threatened by Mary's picketing and the flyers she was handing out.

"There may also have been store employees who would have had difficulty getting another similar-paying job if the store had to let them go or went out of business."

"Jerry, do you think one of the co-owners or employees may have sent the warning letters to Mary?"

"Yes, for sure! Unlike with her proposal for the academy, Mary might, indeed, have decided to abandon her protests due to receiving the letters. The killer likely expected the letters to get Mary to back off and never even considered the possibility of actually killing her until later on."

"Jerry, you make a lot of sense. Let's discuss this some more when I get home."

After dinner, Amy had some additional news for her husband. "Aaron came through for me. I'm meeting with Laura tomorrow at noon at the Ferman Country Diner."

"Sweetheart, that's good news. Do you view Laura as a murder suspect?"

"Sadly, yes. I want to be able to remove her—as well as the other co-owner and the employees—from my list of suspects, but I doubt that can happen, even after the interview."

Jeremy spent several seconds in deep thought, then he revealed his idea, "Why didn't Laura and her partner just refund Mary's purchase money so as to get rid of her? That seems to be the best strategy to preserve their business."

She smiled and nodded. "Jerry, I think you're sure as hell right about that! It will be one of the first questions I'll ask Laura tomorrow."

Thursday, June 7, 2018

At eleven fifty-five, when Amy entered the Country Diner, she was immediately recognized—due to her red scarf—by Laura DeRoy, who was sitting on a couch in the lobby. Laura introduced herself, they shook hands, agreed to use first names, and were escorted by the hostess to a booth.

Laura was in her forties, tall and thin, with a serious face and short brown hair. She wore a dark gray pants suit. Amy thought Laura would, indeed, be the perfect choice to play the role of a businesswoman on TV or in a movie. Right after they ordered their food and drinks, Laura initiated the conversation.

"Amy, I checked you out on the web. You are one of the best private murder investigators around, the cream of the crop. So I'm gonna come right out and tell it to you exactly like it is.

"I had nothing to do with the murder of Mary Rackner. I am also certain that my business partner, Elaine Lanier, whom I've known since college, had nothing to do with it. I hope you can identify the killer and bring him or her to justice. But—God forgive me—I was delighted when Mary was murdered, and I'm deeply grateful to whomever did it." Amy gasped.

"Amy, I'm sorry if I've shocked you. From what I've read in the newspapers, the killer seems to have been someone connected with the Ferman Academy who was angry about Mary's proposal to put greater emphasis on math and English and less on music and art. I don't know if the killer will succeed in stopping the implementation of that proposal, but the killer certainly succeeded in saving our clothing store.

"If Mary had continued picketing and handing out flyers, there's a very good chance she would have bankrupted us and forced us to shut down our store. We were getting ready to sue in court in an effort to force Mary to stop what she was doing. We also planned to sue her for damages. Who knows if we'd have won those cases. By the way, here's one of her flyers." She handed it to Amy, who was ready with Jeremy's question.

"Laura, why didn't you and Elaine just pay Mary the refund money she was demanding—even if she did not deserve it— and thereby get rid of her?"

"Elaine and I had talked about that option. But unless it remained a secret, paying off Mary would have been viewed by the community as a confession that we sold stained and ripped clothing. Our business would likely never recover from that kind of reputation.

"Of course, the whole thing was totally absurd. The idea that not just one, but all six items purchased by Mary on the same visit to the store were badly flawed right from time of purchase is so preposterous that any person of average intelligence would view that claim by Mary as a sick joke. She obviously put those clothes somewhere she shouldn't have put them, and they got ruined.

"Our lawyer suggested the possibility of a settlement where Mary would have her purchases refunded—which would come to about a thousand dollars—and where she would agree to stop protesting and would also sign a nondisclosure agreement to keep the existence of the settlement secret. We were considering that solution, although we feared it would likely somehow be leaked and picked up by the media. Then Mary was murdered, and that ended our nightmare."

"Did you or Elaine send Mary any letters warning her to stop what she was doing?"

Laura shook her head vigorously. "No, of course not. According to the newspaper, it looks the killer sent Mary two anonymous threatening letters in an attempt to get her to withdraw her proposal regarding the academy. Then when Mary stood fast, he or she murdered her as a last desperate resort."

"Were you familiar with Mary and her role as an academy board member prior to all this?"

"No, neither Elaine nor myself had ever heard of her. Of course, once Mary started picketing, we found out all about her and the academy controversy."

They enjoyed their meals, and Amy thanked Laura for meeting with her and for not holding back her feelings. Amy departed and decided to work from home for the rest of the afternoon. When she arrived, she kissed her husband and related her conversation with Laura.

"So Laura put it all out there. She believes that whoever murdered Mary probably saved her store from being shut down, and she's very grateful to him or her for that. She was ready to file a lawsuit against Mary, including asking for monetary damages, but like Aaron, she was not sure whether she would win. She was also considering paying Mary off if Mary would sign a nondisclosure agreement, but she doubted secrecy could actually be maintained."

"Are Laura and Elaine still suspects?"

"Sure, but if she's the killer, Laura put on one hell of a good—and unique—performance. Laura gave me one of the flyers Mary was handing out. I haven't read it yet; let's look at it together." Amy pulled it out of her briefcase and read it aloud:

"Be aware that Ladies Choice finds phony excuses to refuse to honor their seven-day return policy. These shameful actions make them unworthy of our business."

Amy now had a horrified look on her face. "Oh my god, Jerry, that's awful!"

He nodded. "To say it's awful is an understatement. I know you're not a lawyer, but do you think Laura would have won monetary damages in court, or at least gotten a cease-and-desist order against Mary?"

Silence from Amy, who appeared to be in deep thought. After about thirty seconds of contemplation, she rose and went over to her computer, still saying nothing as Jeremy watched her feverously typing on the keyboard and intensely staring at the screen. After about three minutes of computer research, Amy's silence was broken.

"Oh my god, Jerry! Oh my god! I think I've just solved the case!"

"You mean the Mary Rackner murder case?"

"Of course, I mean the Mary Rackner murder case. Everybody made a terribly wrong major assumption—you, me, Christine, Aaron, the police, the media, everybody! The real situation is exactly the reverse of what everyone had thought!"

Jeremy was totally confused. "The reverse? Reverse of what? You are making no sense whatsoever. Do you know who killed Mary? Do you know the motive? And what piece of new information did you suddenly turn up that gave you the solution to the murder?"

"Well, I'm very confident I know who the killer is. I know the motive in general, but not the specifics. And the flyer we just read was my road-to-Damascus moment with regard to solving the case."

"Sweetheart, you are still not making much sense. What do you mean by knowing the general motive but not the specifics? And what could have been on that flyer that gave you the solution to the murder? It was certainly very nasty, but we know Mary was, indeed, on occasion, a very nasty bully."

Amy smiled broadly. "Okay, Jerry, I'll lay it all out for you. The flyer refers to 'shameful actions' by Ladies Choice. Does that sound somewhat familiar?"

"Not really."

"Well, let's go back and look at the warning letter found between the pages of Mary's dictionary." Amy took from her briefcase the sheet of paper that Christine had given her which contained the text, and she read it aloud:

"Hello, Mary. This is the second and final warning letter. You must immediately halt your disgraceful actions, or you will suffer the consequences. You will not know what hit you. To repeat for the last time, stop now or else."

Amy put the sheet back into her briefcase. "Any comments, Jerry?"

He shook his head. "Only that you did show me that letter before, on the day that you first met Christine, and she gave you a copy."

"You have to be a more observant, boy! The letter refers to 'disgraceful actions' by Mary. Now do you see what I'm driving at?"

He shook his head. "Frankly, no."

"Well, you should see it. 'Shameful actions.' 'Disgraceful actions.' That's Mary's style of verbiage. The flyer and the warning letter were *both* written by Mary. It's the exact reverse of what everyone had assumed. Mary did not *receive* any warning letters. Mary *sent* the first warning letter and was deciding whether to send the second letter."

"Sweetheart, do you mean Mary sent the warning letter to herself?"

Amy laughed. "No, silly boy, Mary composed the second warning letter and had not yet sent it out to her intended recipient, who she felt had engaged in 'disgraceful actions.' She put it in her dictionary, probably until she decided whether or not to send it. She had previously sent out the first warning letter to that same recipient.

"That's why the police did not find the first letter or either of the two envelopes in Mary's house. The first letter, plus its envelope, were in the possession of the recipient, and Mary had not yet put the second letter into an envelope, as she was still considering whether to send that letter. Actually, I'm very angry at myself because I should have realized that it was the reverse right from the beginning, when the police could find neither the first warning letter nor either of the two envelopes in Mary's house."

"Sweetheart, it's easy to say now that you should have realized it—and, for that matter, the police should have realized it too—but that's Monday morning quarterbacking, and it's not fair to you or to the police. But wasn't it Mary's clear style to not just send warnings—let alone anonymous warnings? She would openly complain, and she would report the offender's inappropriate activity to the authorities."

She stroked her husband on the cheek. "Jerry, that's the first really smart thing you've said today. And that perceptive observation of yours provides a big clue as to who Mary's recipient must have been. That person must have been a person she otherwise greatly respected, who she did not want to have to publicly disgrace and humiliate.

"She sent the first letter, hoping that the recipient would terminate their objectionable conduct, but the recipient apparently did not do so. Therefore, Mary composed a second warning letter, but she was apparently undecided as to whether to send it out or whether to go public and contact the authorities without sending another letter.

"But, Jerry, there is one more very important thing we know about the recipient of the first letter. And I'm sure you know what that is." She stopped stroking his cheek.

Jeremy shook his head. "I'm sorry, but I have no idea. No, wait a second." Now he laughed. "Of course, I know; the recipient's name has to be Mary!"

Amy briefly resumed her stroking. "Smart boy! I knew you could do it!" They both laughed.

"Sweetheart, do we know of any woman also named Mary whom our Mary respected enough to send an anonymous warning letter and not immediately contact the authorities? And if our Mary respected this other Mary that much, why be anonymous?"

"Jerry, let me answer your second question first. It's very likely that the reason for the anonymity is that the infraction is extremely serious, maybe even criminal—I'll go further, very likely criminal—as opposed to spilling Pepsi onto the road, putting up political posters, or not refunding the purchase price for stained clothes. Mary must have realized that the recipient would not be happy to learn that someone she knew was aware of her serious infraction. It would permanently negatively affect their relationship. So the warning letter was sent anonymously."

He nodded. "That makes sense. The recipient must have been doing something really bad."

"Now, Jerry, to answer your first question. At first glance, we don't know of anyone named Mary whom our Mary greatly respected. But come over to the computer and I'll go onto a 'find nicknames' website and type in 'Mary.' Now look at the fifth nickname on their list."

Jerry took a look. "Oh, wow, Polly! Polly is the name of the chair of the Ferman Academy Board of Trustees! Did you determine if our Polly's actual first name is Mary?"

Amy flashed a broad smile. "As a matter of fact, that's what I just did. I used my favorite people-search website, and they listed Mary Medwick as an alternate name for Polly Medwick of Ferman Township. That's good enough for me.

"So here's my scenario for what happened. Polly was doing something awful on a continuing basis. Somehow, Mary found out about this. Mary liked and respected Polly. She was shocked by Polly's behavior, but she didn't want to humiliate Polly, end Polly's service on the board, permanently ruin their relationship, and maybe cause Polly to end up in prison. She decided to send Polly an anonymous warning letter in the hope that Polly would end the behavior. But apparently Polly did not end the behavior. Mary prepared a second letter, but she was undecided as to whether to send it out to Polly or whether to come out and publicly report Polly's behavior.

"While Mary was agonizing about this difficult decision, Polly somehow discovered that it was Mary who had sent the anonymous warning letter and who, therefore, was aware of Polly's behavior. Polly decided that for Mary to be aware of what was going on was simply too much of a risk—let alone for Mary to publicly reveal Polly's conduct—so the only feasible solution for her was to kill Mary.

"Polly either acquired or already possessed a handgun, equipped with a silencer. She went to Mary's house on April 14 and shot and killed Mary while her victim was napping in her backyard. Polly probably wore gloves to make sure there were no prints or DNA. She threw the gun into the pool. Then she left, without realizing that she had made two shoe prints with her unusual shoes, which are apparently only available in three Adriatic countries."

"Sweetheart, why would our Mary have addressed her anonymous letters to Mary, rather than Polly?"

Amy spent a few seconds pondering her husband's question. Then she responded, "My guess is that Mary wanted Polly to think her warning letters came from someone who knew her as Mary. That would eliminate board members like Mary from suspicion, as they knew her as Polly. Obviously, that strategy by Mary ultimately did not work."

Jeremy nodded. "Makes sense. But I have a simpler explanation. Mary cut out her words from two editions of the *New York Post*. She probably found the word 'Mary' in one of those newspapers, but not the word 'Polly.' So rather than go through the hassle of cutting out the five letters separately, she just cut out the intact word 'Mary,' which she knew was Polly's actual name."

She nodded. "Yeah, you could be right. But I'm still going with my explanation."

"So what do you do now that you are convinced that Polly is the murderer?"

"Well, the police cannot search Polly's house without probable cause. So as it stands now, the Adriatic shoes and Mary's first warning letter are unreachable, assuming they're located somewhere in Polly's house. So my only option seems to be to ask Mr. Murray to recruit some Spy4U people who will do discrete surveillance of Polly and, hopefully, determine what kind of terrible thing she's been doing. If Polly is doing something illegal, and if we can produce evidence of this and provide it to the police, then they'll probably have enough to search her house."

"Sweetheart, what if Polly's offense is unethical and embarrassing but not illegal? What do we do then?"

Amy smiled. "Then we may have to report everything we have to Captain Zorkin of the Ferman Police—and also sometime soon after that, to Christine. And then the police will decide where to go from there—maybe nowhere. Polly may get away with murder."

"Can't you find some way to trick Polly into producing or wearing the Adriatic shoes and thereby incriminating herself?"

"Maybe, but I wouldn't bet on succeeding in pulling that off. However, who knows? It would certainly be worth a try, if I can cook up some kind of scam."

"Sweetheart, what kind of awful conduct could Polly have been undertaking that would cause her to murder Mary because Mary found out?"

Amy smiled. "My best guess is that it would have to involve drugs or sex. Polly has never been married. I'll bet two-to-one on sex, but don't ask me to elaborate further, because I have no idea."

Friday, June 8, 2018

Amy was waiting outside Chester's office when he arrived for work at 9:15 a.m. "Amy, you seem very excited; come on in and tell me what's going on."

They took seats in his office, and Amy explained to her boss, in detail, how she came to the conclusion that Polly Medwick had murdered Mary Rackner and why Spy4U should initiate a surveillance of Polly in an attempt to determine the nature of her bad conduct and, hopefully, obtain some video or audio evidence of that conduct.

"So, Mr. Murray, as far as I can see this surveillance is our best hope—and may be our only hope—to bring Polly to justice for the murder."

Chester smiled. "First, I want to shake your hand; congratulations on solving the case!" He walked over to Amy's chair, and Amy grasped his extended right hand; then he sat back down. "I have been looking at the media coverage of Mary's murder. Everyone simply assumed that someone had been sending Mary warning letters. You managed to go against the entire crowd, think way outside the box, and get to the truth. That's quite an achievement!"

"Mr. Murray, I wish I could pretend I was all that, but it was just a matter of comparing the text of Mary's handouts in front of the clothing store to the leaked text of the second warning letter. As I told Jerry, I actually should have realized everything a long time ago, when the police did not find the first warning letter and also found no envelopes."

He shook his head vigorously. "Amy, only for you was it a matter of comparing those two texts. For everyone else, it was an unsolvable case. As I told you before—I think it was regarding the Lido Deck case—don't you dare ever tell anyone that solving your case was an easy task, because it would never have been easy—and often would have been impossible—for anyone else. You are indeed one in a million!" Amy's face was turning bright red.

"And I also have a little surprise for you. It's from Richard Smith, as his extra thanks for determining the identity of the culprit who misused Richard's credit card number to make campaign donations."

He handed Amy an envelope from which she removed a check. "Oh my god, three thousand dollars!"

Chester nodded. "I had told Richard that any bonus was up to him, and it would all go to you, rather than the usual fifty-fifty split between you and Spy4U. Anyhow, of course I'll set up surveillance of Polly Medwick, including video and audio. Obviously, if there is, indeed, bad behavior to find, it may take some time for us to find it. So you may have to be patient."

Amy nodded. "Of course, no problem." The meeting ended, and Amy went back to her office and phoned her husband.

"Jerry, Jerry! Mr. Murray just gave me a check for $3,000 as my bonus from Richard Smith for solving his credit card fraud case. No fifty-fifty split! The whole bonus went to me."

"Wow! Are you gonna use some of the money to buy anything special?"

"Yeah, I'll use some of that money to have them put a double portion of pepperoni on a pepperoni and meatball pizza for you to bring home for dinner this evening. Oh, and also use some of my bonus money to purchase a triple chocolate cake from Fern's Bakery and then bring it home for dessert.

Her husband laughed. "Okay, sweetheart, will do."

Thursday, June 14, 2018

At 2:45 p.m., Chester knocked on Amy's office door, and she invited him in. He took the seat across the desk from where Amy was sitting. "It took us a bit of time to verify some information, but, Amy, I think we've got her."

"Oh my god, Mr. Murray, oh my god! Can you give me the details?"

He smiled. "You bet, that's exactly what I'm here to do. At 5:00 p.m. this past Saturday, Polly Medwick left her house and drove to a Walmart parking lot around ten miles from Ferman Township. She parked next to a Subaru. A middle-aged woman escorted a tall, thin teenage boy from the Subaru to Polly's Toyota. The teenager sat in the front passenger seat, and Polly drove away with the teenager. A minute or two later, the Subaru also left the lot.

"We followed the Subaru to a small bungalow in a not-so-hot neighborhood in Reeves Township, about fifteen miles from Ferman and five miles from the Walmart. The middle-aged woman entered the building, which appeared to be her home, and stayed there until eleven thirty on Sunday morning, when she drove back to the same Walmart parking lot and picked up the teenager, who had just exited with Polly from Polly's Toyota. Both cars then drove back to their respective homes."

Amy interrupted. "So where did Polly and the teenage boy go from roughly five-thirty Saturday afternoon until she brought the teenager back at around noon?"

"They went to a garden apartment in Maywood that Polly had likely rented mainly for this purpose. From the time they entered the apartment, at roughly six in the evening on Saturday, they did not leave until around eleven thirty on Sunday morning.

"We checked out the people at the address of the destination to which the Subaru was driven. The boy is Allen Moro. He's fifteen years old and will be sixteen in October. In addition, he's mentally impaired. The middle-aged woman is Doris Moro, his mother—his single mother. Allen is her only child. Unless I miss my guess, Doris is receiving cash payments every month from Polly. That would help to explain everything.

"There is nothing of interest to report regarding Polly since noon on Sunday. I suggest that we maintain the surveillance over this coming weekend and see if the same events are repeated that occurred on the previous weekend."

Amy nodded. "Good idea. I'll bet the same thing happens, with regard to Polly and Allen, during the majority of weekends. In any case, I can now guess how Mary likely discovered what Polly was doing. She probably just happened to be shopping at that Walmart on a Saturday, in the late afternoon, and she happened to be close enough in the parking lot to get a good view of the transfer of Allen between cars.

"Also, sometime after receiving the warning letter, Polly probably realized that Mary was the letter sender when she observed Mary shopping at that Walmart, or maybe even seeing Mary nearby in the parking lot when a transfer was going on."

Chester nodded. "Sounds plausible. Of course, Mary may have given herself away by the way she looked at Polly when they saw each other at that Walmart, or maybe elsewhere."

Now Amy nodded. "Yes, that certainly is a possibility. Mr. Murray, did they get any audio or video evidence of what happened last weekend?"

"Oh yes, there's good video of everything. As I said, I think we've got her."

When Amy got home, she told her husband she had fantastic news, but first she wanted them to enjoy the Chinese takeout that he'd brought home for dinner. After the meal, she related what Chester had told her, plus her ideas regarding how Mary found out about Polly and then how Polly found out about Mary.

"Sweetheart, that is, indeed, absolutely fantastic! Polly is toast. She'll be going to jail for endangering the welfare of a minor plus statutory rape and maybe some other stuff too. And if they find the Adriatic shoes at her house in the search they will now be able to do, Polly will likely be sent away for murder. When will you meet with Captain Zorkin?"

"Almost certainly some time next week, hopefully after we obtain video of a second weekend where Polly and Allen pair up."

"How do you think this relationship between Polly and Allen got started?"

Amy smiled. "Well, Polly told me she still does some private tutoring. I would presume that Allen's mother hired Polly to help her mentally impaired son with some aspect of English, and it proceeded from there."

He nodded. "Makes perfect sense. When will you lay it all out for Christine?"

"I'll wait till Polly is arrested regarding her illicit behavior with Allen, which is now a virtual certainty. Then I'll see whether they end up with enough to charge Polly with murder. At that point, even if there is no murder charge, I expect to report our findings to Christine. I'll verify this plan with Mr. Murray. So for now, we'll just wait and see what happens this weekend.

"Oh, and before I forget, there's one more piece of news. At around four o'clock, I got a call from Oscar Lewis, Jasper's lawyer. He told me that Jasper had died on June sixth. And he told me about Jasper's will.

"Mary inherited everything, and if, for any reason, she could not inherit, then Jasper's money is evenly split between three charities."

"So, sweetheart, based on what Oscar told you, his nieces never had any chance to inherit."

She smiled. "Jerry, you're sure as hell right about that."

"And Denise was correct when she insisted to you that the warning letter coming just before the murder was definitely not a coincidence and was very significant with regard to solving the murder."

"Right again, Jerry; Denise was spot-on, and you're two for two."

Monday, June 18, 2018

At 10:15 a.m., Amy's office phone rang. It was Chester. "Amy, I've been told by our people that this past weekend was a nearly exact repetition of the previous weekend. And as previously, we have all the new video. You should now make an appointment to see the police captain."

She thanked her boss for all his assistance and made the phone call to the Ferman PD. Then she phoned Jeremy and told him what Chester said, and that she was meeting with Captain Zorkin at three o'clock in Ferman Township.

"So, sweetheart, now it's all up to the Ferman police, right?"

"Right, Jerry, and I'll come home straight from my meeting with Mark. Let's celebrate with dinner at Big Tony's."

At five past three, Captain Mark Zorkin welcomed Amy into his office, and they both took seats. "So, Amy, I presume you're here because you have some additional questions for me to help with your murder investigation."

"Sorry, Mark, you presume wrong. We have identified the killer and the motive. We also believe that we have enough evidence to allow you to search the killer's home and, hopefully, find the shoes that made the prints in Mary's backyard. We all made a major assumption in this case that turned out to be incorrect. The actual facts were the reverse of our assumption."

The captain had a stunned look on his face as Amy carefully went over the step-by-step process whereby Polly was identified as the killer. When Amy was done, she presented him with the videos of Polly with Allen. Now Mark's appearance changed from stunned to shocked. His mouth was wide open.

"Amy, you are absolutely unbelievable!"

"Mark," she interrupted, "it was a Spy4U team effort, particularly the surveillance of Polly and the videos. That's just one of the many reasons why I'm so proud to work at Spy4U."

He nodded. "Okay, Amy, I get what you're saying. And I'll repeat, you are absolutely unbelievable! Thank you for solving the murder when we were stymied. And if we can make an arrest for the murder, which I think is now a strong possibility, then you've also made me and the entire Ferman PD look good."

"Mark, if I can make you and the Ferman PD look good, I'll be thrilled. Thank you for all the assistance you have provided."

At dinner, Amy and Jeremy enjoyed thick steaks and agreed that Big Tony—who often personally greeted all dinner patrons— was even more corpulent than when they last ate at his restaurant. "So, Jerry, you're the probability expert. What are the odds that the police can arrest Polly for murder?"

He laughed. "That's not actually a question a probability expert can answer any better than anyone else. But I'd say it's a decent chance. We'll just have to wait and see."

"Jerry, you're sure as hell right about that."

Thursday, June 21, 2018

At six in the evening, while Amy and Jeremy were eating dinner at their apartment, Amy's phone rang. "Hi, Amy, this is Mark; it's all over." Amy put on the speaker. "We got the search warrant for Polly's house. No warning letter, she must have gotten rid of it. But we did find the shoes. Polly has been arrested for murder, as well as for endangering the welfare of a minor. I've been told there may also be a charge of statutory rape."

Amy thanked the captain for letting her know and then got off the phone. "Jerry, I don't feel sorry for Polly; should I?"

He shook his head. "Polly's behavior regarding Allen was truly horrible. But as awful as it was, if that was the only blotch on her long and admirable career, then yes, I'd say you could possibly feel sorry for her. But murdering Mary? As I see it, there's no longer any room for sympathy."

"Yeah, I guess you're right. I now have to phone Christine and give her the whole story—of course Spy4U will also send her a written report. After that, I should also call Morton and Aaron—and probably some others—to give them the news and thank them for their assistance. And, of course, my first call right now is to Mr. Murray." She punched in Chester's number.

"Hi, it's Amy. Sorry to bother you at dinnertime, but the police captain just called and said Polly has been arrested for both murder and endangering the welfare of a minor."

"That's fantastic! Again, congratulations!"

Amy got off the phone, and her husband had a question. "Sweetheart, what if after killing Mary, Polly had seen the dirt from the backyard on her Adriatic shoes and for that reason, decided, as a precaution, to get rid of those shoes—just like she apparently got rid of Mary's first warning letter. In that case, do you think Polly would have gotten away with the murder?"

Amy closed her eyes and spent some time in deep thought; then she spoke. "Jerry, you and I and the police would have known that Polly was the killer, but would there have been enough evidence, without the shoes, to indict Polly for murder, let alone convict her? I doubt it. Maybe the police will find something else which is sufficiently incriminating, with regard to her cell phone, her computer, or her gloves—of course, she probably got rid of the gloves she wore while shooting Mary. Or maybe they'll find some incriminating stuff elsewhere. But my best guess is no; Polly would be going to jail for the other charges, involving Allen, but probably not for the murder."

"Sweetheart, Mary had two completely different personalities, like Dr. Jekyll and Mr. Hyde. With some people, she was a nasty bully, and with others, she was always friendly and pleasant. It's weird."

She nodded. "That's a good point. For example, look at Christine's, Aaron's, and Anna's experiences with Mary, compared to those of Doreen, Wendy, and Laura."

He smiled. "The really dumb thing Polly did was to not accept the way out that Mary had clearly offered her. If, after receiving the warning letter, Polly had terminated her relationship with Allen, she likely could have gone on with her life as a respected figure in the community. And I'll bet she could have found an older guy—or maybe even a guy in his twenties looking for a sugar momma—to satisfy her sexual needs.

"Of course, in that case, Polly could never be sure that Mary would not, at some point, change her mind and report Polly to the authorities."

Amy laughed. "Jerry, you're sure as hell right about that!"

THE END

About the Author

David Schwinger is retired, having spent his entire career teaching mathematics at City College, City University of New York. He now lives in Florida with his wife, Sherryl, whom he met when she was his student. In addition to having written fifteen Amy Bell murder mysteries, David composes songs and plays pickleball. He and Sherryl have traveled to over 130 countries. David began his mystery-writing career in 2013, upon the urging of his wife. *The Teacher's Pet Murders*, his first book, was inspired by the secret romantic relationship David had with Sherryl while she was his student at City College. In that book, his vivacious and brilliant heroine/detective, Amy Bell, made her first appearance. Amy has continued to use her extraordinary talents to solve murders in all of David's succeeding books.